DEAD ED

MIKE POLIZZI

Cover Art by
CHERI NOWAK

ISBN: 978-0-6152-1323-1

ARKANVILLE PRESS

www.mikepolizzi.com

Long Island

Printed in The United States of America

For
April

AUTHOR'S NOTE

I am not an English major. I've studied and practiced filmmaking for the past 20-years. Therefore, *movies* are my language and that is why you may find this particular story to read more like a screenplay than one of those wordy, lengthy novels. So, to the horror fan/movie buff reading this, you're in luck! And, to any person who does not have the time or patience for a *slow-moving book*, you're in luck too! "Dead Ed" is a fast-paced, thrilling, dark and dramatic tale – which I originally imagined in 1998. Finally, after 10-years of fine-tuning, *here it is!* Enjoy!

WARNING: This book contains Adult Language, Some Sexuality and Violence. *In other words: this is rated R!*

Mike Polizzi,
Long Island, NY
April 2008

DEAD ED

PROLOGUE:
ASYLUM

When professor Viktor Drodz was admitted into the Cromwell Psychiatric Center in 1984 he inadvertently became a vital point of interest to one of the ward's most enthusiastic interns. His name was William Praetor and he was in his second year of college at the time, with expectations to become a psychiatrist one day. But, he was also very fond of biology, which Drodz was formerly a professor of. He actually had him for class one brief semester, before the breakdown, and it pleased him to pick his brain once in a while.

For years, Praetor was uncertain as to what actually caused his unfortunate mentor's collapse. But, nevertheless, he made an effort to have at least one conversation with him every day he worked there.

Their bonding eventually formed into an inspiring friendship. It was like a father/son connection, as Drodz always shared his knowledge and stories with Praetor. But, still, nothing was ever related or referred to the events that put Drodz in a padded cell. At least, not until around 1997, when *Dr. William Praetor* became his exclusive psychiatrist.

Drodz's personal life became Praetor's career. It was all very interesting, but what really captivated him the most was Drodz's *dark secret* – the secret that sentenced him in that asylum for life.

"Tell me more about this Lewis Sypher person," Praetor asked Drodz, during one of their sessions in 1999.

Drodz sighed, and then sunk into his seat. The name made him feel uncomfortable and Praetor knew it. "What is there to say?" Drodz asked, in his coarse, Romanian accent. "His name says it all."

"Yes, I understand the encryption of his name. But, prior to his affair with your wife, what exactly did he offer you?"

"I thought I mentioned this to you before, William. He shared his knowledge of chemistry."

"I understand, Viktor, but I'm afraid that explanation is too vague. If you trust me as your doctor, you have an obligation to be as precise as possible. That's the only way I could help you get out of here. You would like to see your daughter again, wouldn't you?"

For the first time in years, Drodz actually felt a shed of hope. "You could do that for me?"

"Of course. But, you're going to have to be co-operative. As long as you continue to answer honestly and thoroughly, I could get you out of here within the next ten years."

"William, you are a saint. How could I repay such a generous offer?"

"Simply. Just answer my questions truthfully and we'll call it even."

"I cannot argue with that. But, I warn you: you may not believe what I tell you."

"We'll leave that verdict to me. Now, what did you need those chemicals for?"

Drodz hesitated, and then confessed: "They were used for a cure."

"A cure for what?"

Drodz hesitated again. "Life is too short, William. Death is unnecessary... It was a cure for death."

CHAPTER 1:
AWAKENING

What happens when we die?

A common question that we all ask ourselves at least once in our lifetime. It's right up there with *"where do we come from?"* and *"why are we here?"*

Some say that religions were formed to answer these questions and set our minds at ease. It's human nature to guess, wonder and question; and it's human nature to presume a logical explanation.

Some believe that when you die, your soul travels to Heaven or Hell – or Purgatory. Others believe that you return to life as something – *or someone* – completely different. And, there are those who believe that we just simply expire and become nothing – as we were before we were born.

Then you have the whole ghost theory – *or is it reality?*

There's no denying that there are things in this world that the human eye cannot see. We cannot see all that is microscopic; we cannot see viruses floating in the air; and we cannot see the spirits of the dead.

Nevertheless, there are a small percentage of people that have the ability to "glance" at the paranormal universe beside us. Edward Talbot was reluctantly one of them.

* * *

"Edward," said a rasping voice. *"Come with us."*

These words reached Edward Talbot's 4-year-old ears while he began to fall asleep on the sofa. But, he didn't recognize the voice speaking to him.

It was only 3 o'clock in the afternoon and he had been watching cartoons ever since his mother, Nora, had picked him up from daycare. He began to doze off in the living room shortly after, while his mother prepared dinner in the kitchen.

They were the only two people in the apartment. His father, Ed, Sr., was still at work. *So, who the hell was calling Ed's name?*

Around the corner from the television set was a hall that led to two bedrooms, the bathroom and a closet. The unfamiliar voice extended from this area and when little Ed slowly, and placidly, adjusted his vision, he saw two distorted torsos hovering approximately three feet above the hallway floor. They stood side-by-side and stared directly at Ed.

He knew that whatever his subconscious witnessed was unnatural. They were a couple of sustained fog patches with dark openings that resembled a mouth and a pair of eyes.

The one on the left gestured Ed with an arm-like appendage. "Come with us," it repeated.

The shock caused Ed's prime-conscious to prevail and the reality of what stood before him was finally verified. His face turned as white as a sheet. A sudden outburst of sweat seeped through every single pore in his body. His heartbeat became so rapid that he heard the pounding from his chest. His muscles tightened with stress and locked his joints.

But, in a short moment, Ed managed to conquer the psychological restraint and bolted into the kitchen. He leaped into the arms of his mother and almost caused her to drop a tin tray of raw chicken legs.

"Edward," she cried. "What's the matter?"

With his eyes still wide open – and never blinking – he managed to force out the words, "There are people in the-the hall!"

Nora knew that her son was imagining things, so she told him that it was only a dream. Ed wasn't convinced, but his naïve mind was easily manipulated by her suggestion. He soon forgot about it, but when he returned to the sofa he spent the rest of the day taking an occasional glance at the empty hall.

Eventually, the cartoons distracted Ed fully... That is, until a monstrous hand tore through the sofa cushion and seized him!

He screamed on the top of his lungs so loud that all of Manhattan could hear. But, for some bizarre reason, nobody did – not even his mother. She did not flinch nor speak. It was as if Ed was not there at all.

A digital alarm clock had miraculously appeared on the coffee table. It rang so loud that it actually overrode Ed's continual petrified scream.

A dream, Nora had suggested earlier. Perhaps it was... *a dream within a dream.*

* * *

Ed awoke in a startle to the sound of his irritating alarm clock.

Beside him lied his wife, Lena. She was still exhausted, but managed to reach over to the night table and turned off the irritating alarm clock. Ed acknowledged that it was 7 o'clock in the morning, but he couldn't bring himself to realize that it was Monday all over again. Another weekend came and went in a blink of an eye.

Life was going way too fast. The reality of just having a birthday on October 6th, and having one foot in the grave at 43-years-old, was not a comforting thought for Ed, nor was it one he could forget.

Lena kept her eyes shut, as she attempted to snooze for another ten minutes, but she sensed Ed remaining perfectly still in thought. "Another nightmare?" she asked him, groggily, and then she felt the bed shake a bit as he nodded. "Same one?"

"Yeah," he sighed.

"What do you think it means?"

Ed had no idea what the hell it meant. But, having the same dream for the past week was getting pretty frustrating for him.

He hesitated, before he gave his snoozing wife a reply. He chose to forget about it. "It means," he told her, as he leaned over her beautiful face to kiss it, "that I have to get ready for work." He climbed out of bed and stepped into their private bathroom to urinate.

As he stood over the toilet for a moment, he peered out the tiny window and stared at his 2-acre backyard – *his canvas*, if you will. And, on this canvas he had painted four work sheds, a gazebo and a two-door garage. He did this all over a period of fifteen years. It kept him busy on the weekends, when he wasn't being a boring life insurance broker – and, carpentry had been a passionate hobby of his since high school.

But, his real passion existed inside the two-door garage. His babies. We're talking ten motorcycles here. Ten loud, slick machines on wheels that made him feel twenty-years younger – the age he was when he purchased his first bike.

Lena resented the fact that he even had them – she foreboded Ed to ride them, but she was quite fond of the value of the cycles. Once in a while, she allowed him to ride, but it wasn't enough.

After emptying his bladder, he decided to refill it with some orange juice, but something had caught his attention when he passed the living room. That *something* was his 18-year-old daughter, Crystal, who was sound asleep in front of the blaring television, and next to her boyfriend, Owen Murphy. They were in a cuddled position, which made Ed feel a little uncomfortable. Even though Crystal had been dating Owen exclusively for a year, Ed wasn't too sure if he was fond of him yet. So, Ed quietly nudged his lovely daughter away from Owen's unconscious grip. He then turned the TV off and carried on with his morning ritual.

By the time Ed returned to the master bedroom, Lena was already showered and at her make-up table, drying her hair. He tried to speak to her, but the screaming hairdryer made her oblivious to his presence. She eventually startled when she noticed his lips flapping in the mirror, and then turned off the dryer for a moment. "I'm sorry, what?" she asked him.

"I said: are you okay with Owen sleeping over?"

"He slept over?"

"Uh, yeah."

"Oh, they must've dozed off watching that horror movie marathon," she assumed, as Ed returned to their private bathroom to shower and shave – simultaneously. He even left the door open, so he could continue the conversation.

But, during that time, she had received two text-messages back-to-back and checked them.

"Somebody's impatient," Ed remarked, in reference to the message chimes.

"It's just Dina from work."

"Again? She's been texting you like that since Labor Day."

"So, what?"

"So, can't she just *wait* to talk to you at the office?"

"What can I tell ya, babe. She's crazy."

Ed shrugged it off, and then returned to his previous thoughts. "Hey, I'm surprised Owen's tongue wasn't stuck in Crystal's throat," he said, in annoyance.

"Oh, come on, Ed, they're in love," she said, while typing a reply text-message.

"They're too young to be in love."

"They're eighteen."

"Exactly."

"*We* were in high school!"

Ed was stumped for a moment – Lena was correct. "Alright, shut up," he told her, as she chuckled back at him. He decided to change the subject, but Lena had already turned her hairdryer back on. When he realized that she couldn't hear him anymore, he spent the rest of his shower time staring out that tiny, steamed up window and daydreamed.

* * *

Ed remembered when he and Lena fell in love – he thought it would help make him feel less uptight and more understanding about Crystal's relationship with Owen.

As he reminisced, he appreciated the fact that if he and his parents never relocated from Manhattan to the eastern north shore suburbs of Long Island when he was thirteen, he would've never met Lena King.

It was the beginning of their junior year of high school and, on a cold day during their gym class; the boys and girls shared the track to run *the mile*. Ed had always been in average shape, but was never fond of forced labor. Therefore, he also disliked obligated exercise, like running the track four times around. But, he did it anyway. Unfortunately, between the cold air and the panting, Ed began to have a coughing fit, which then caused him to slow down.

Lena wasn't too far behind him and, being the compassionate person that her born-again minister father raised her to be, she approached Ed, whom was a complete stranger. She asked him if he was all right, but he could only answer with dry heaves. The uncontrollable postnasal drip suddenly caused him to spew his breakfast and the panting caused him to collapse.

Later, Ed was ironically diagnosed with exercise-induced asthma, which got him out of gym class for the remainder of high school. But, that didn't stop him from visiting Lena, who won his heart over sheer kindness.

By the time they both reached the age of twenty, Ed popped the big question. She, of course, happily accepted, and before they knew it, they shacked up in their lovely ranch in the middle of Long Island's best kept secret – Arkanville, New York.

* * *

Arkanville is a wooded suburb – a small quiet town near the Long Island Sound. In fact, Main Street – the central strip of the town, where you would find the pizzeria, deli, coffee shop and pub – leads to a quaint park that overlooks a beautiful view of the water. Literally to be found at the end of Main Street, this park is where all of locals like to go in the warmer weather.

Lena and Ed used to picnic in this park quite often – back when times were more romantic for them. But, those times faded away when Crystal was born.

Crystal wasn't exactly a planned pregnancy. Lena would've preferred to have children when she reached thirty-years-old. She wanted to live out her twenty-something years freely and selfishly, without the responsibilities of being a parent.

Abortion and adoption were both out of the question. Nobody – including their parents – approved those options. So, naturally, she had Crystal nine-months later.

But, Lena had actually suffered a great deal when she was in labor. Unfortunately, baby Crystal was awkwardly positioned in her womb and the physicians were unable to remove her normally. She had to have a Caesarean done and nearly died in the process.

But, when Lena rejuvenated, she vowed to Ed that Crystal was going to be the only child they'd ever have. Ed was slightly disappointed; he would've liked to have more children. But, it wasn't going to happen, so he had no choice but to accept that disappointing fact.

Ed adored Crystal very much. As a matter of fact, he was both her father and her mother for a while. Lena elected Ed as the weekend baby-sitter, so that she could go out socializing with her friends.

Crystal became a daddy's girl - they were buddies and Ed had no complaints about that.

Of course, Lena had eventually grew out of her selfish phase, and then landed a career as a Wills and Estates Attorney - a profession that she had spent eight-years schooling for; but her heart was only in it for the money.

Ed, on the other hand, was already an established Broker in the Life Insurance industry.

Together, they took home a decent dollar. But, as luck would have it, Ed was the one with the big bucks in the family - between his salary, his retirement savings, his assets and his one million dollar life insurance policy.

In addition, he had a very generous Will, which Lena drafted for him.

It was safe to say that the Talbots lived very comfortably.

CHAPTER 2:
CATCHING UP WITH GARY

Ed's office was on the second floor of a corporate building in the heart of an industrial park – only a five-minute drive from home.

His office was kept neatly organized. Framed photos of his wife and daughter rested on the corner of his desk, beside his 17″ flat-screen computer monitor – which he had switched on as soon as he sat down.

He checked his email only to find a weekend's worth of unwanted pornography, pills for crotch dysfunction and Caribbean vacation scams. He deleted them all immediately, and then opened his electronic calendar, which revealed several appointments for the month.

It was Monday, October 27, 2008 and he was scheduled to see Ms. Jade Barker at 10:00AM – a random referral whom he had never met before.

In a matter of seconds, he received a few more junk emails. He grunted, "Damn it, Gary," and then deleted them.

Gary Walker was in the habit of surfing the Internet at work for naked women and twisted videos of elderly women who get dragged across plateaus by dogs. He was only a few years younger than Ed, yet he acted like an adolescent wiseass.

Gary was a perverted womanizer, yet somehow managed to be handsome and charming. Women would usually never decline his invitations. But, by the third date they would notice his absurdity and then dump him.

Evidently, Gary always chose an unusual or obscene website over a meaningful love life.

That morning, Gary couldn't wait to share his new discovery with Ed. When he greeted him, he practically shoved Ed off his own computer and took control of it. "Hey, buddy," Gary began, "you wanna see something cool?"

Ed was thrown off by his friend's persistence, but let the annoyance roll off his shoulder. "I don't know, Gary; if it's a woman getting ravaged by a donkey I'm not interested."

Gary entered a website which revealed a 30-year-old rugged geek who called himself "Mysterious Lee." The content and images related to the supernatural – haunted houses, mostly.

"Who's 'Mysterious Lee?'" Ed asked.

"Remember that client I had to see on Friday – the 77-year-old Brit who thought he could buy life insurance? Christopher Cushing?"

"Vaguely. I had a long weekend; last week hasn't completely returned to my memory yet."

"Well, this is his grandson: Lee Cushing."

"And why should I be impressed?"

"What, are you blind? Look, man! The guy's a paranormal investigator! You can ask him about that experience you had when you were a kid."

"Gary, that was just a nightmare I had when I was 4-years-old. My imagination was deceiving."

"Bullshit! You told me it was real – and you even told me you still have nightmares about it."

"It felt real – and I was on my fourth Scotch when I told you that, by the way."

"What happened again?"

"I was half asleep on my parents' couch and saw these two foggy images in the hallway."

"And?"

"And, they kept calling my name and waving me over to them."

"And, you felt glued to the sofa for a while, before you were able to break free and jump into your mother's arms," Gary added, and then Ed sighed. "Ed,

I've taken the liberty to do a little research on your parents' old Upper West Side apartment. A couple had actually died there in 1955 – right before your father bought it. You had an encounter, my friend – and this Lee character could verify that for you."

"You're never gonna let this go, are ya?"

"Nope."

"When are you meeting with this Mystery Lee?"

"Mysterious Lee. He's actually meeting me for lunch today. Join us."

Before Ed could answer, a young, striking blonde – Gary's new assistant – interrupted them. "Excuse me, gentlemen," she said. "You have a 10 o'clock, Gary."

"Yes, thank you, Amy," Gary smiled, and then intently watched her walk away. He turned back to Ed, still grinning. "Do you think they'll fire me if I fool around with her?"

"I think you've broken enough hearts, Gary."

Gary chuckled, and then glanced at his watch. "Well, I have a 10 o'clock."

"Yeah, me too."

"I'll see you at lunch. Usual place."

"Fine."

"You'll thank me later."

CHAPTER 3:
JADED

Jade Barker was an alluring brunette in her late-twenties. She greeted Ed at her front door, wearing only a towel around her slender body.

Her hair was damp, so Ed could only presume that she had just gotten out of the shower. He felt awkward about it, but couldn't help to feel a little attracted to her.

She didn't say a word at first, but her face said it all. She was annoyed and Ed knew why.

"G-Good morning, Ms. Barker," Ed stuttered. "I'm Ed Talbot, we spoke on the phone last week."

"You were supposed to be here twenty minutes

ago."

"I apologize for that. I was tied up at the office." Tied up from grabbing a cup of coffee on his way out was more like it.

"May I come in and just explain a few things to you real quick? Or, would you like to reschedule? I see that you're..."

"No, it's alright. I have to get ready for work, but come on in."

She led him inside and shut the door.

Her house was a bit unusual. Everything was drab and morbid – black furniture, gothic paintings, a shelf occupied with books on witchcraft and the occult. Ed almost felt uncomfortable being in this house. But, he was a professional and this was a business matter.

"Make yourself at home," she told him, as she disappeared into her bedroom to get dressed. But, the last thing Ed wanted to do was make himself at home – not in this freak house. "So, what do you have to offer?" she asked him, from her bedroom.

"Well, I don't want to bore you with details, but there are several types of life insurance that you can choose from."

"Do you have discount life insurance?"

Ed chuckled, "Your finances may be tight, I'm sure, but life insurance isn't where I would skim."

"Where would you skim?"

"Oh, I don't know... Generic cereal, generic food, don't get the premium channels..." He spotted a dime bag of marijuana on the floor, and then picked it up. "And, I would cut back on the recreational spending."

Jade returned from her bedroom, dressed in black, trendy clothes. "What do you mean?" she asked, and then she noticed her merchandise in Ed's hand. "Oh." She approached Ed and snatched her property back. "This isn't gonna count against me, is it?"

"We'll just say it's for your glaucoma."

Jade was surprised. She looked Ed up and down, and then smirked. "That's pretty cool of you, mister..."

He completed her sentence: "Ed."

"Well, that's original," she chuckled.

"You can just call me Ed," he smiled. "No 'mister.'"

"Would you like a drink, Ed?"

"Sure. What do you have?"

"Beer and water."

"Water, thank you."

As Jade went to the kitchen to grab a couple of drinks, Ed tried to remain focused. "So, do you have any close relatives?" he asked her. "A spouse, perhaps?" Jade returned to him with only two bottles of beer in hand. Ed was confused when she handed him one. "This is a first."

"What?"

"I never drank beer in the morning before."

"It's much better than water," she said, smiling, as she watched him take a swig of the beer. "So, what were you asking me?"

"Well, I was wondering if you were going to make this policy out to a significant other."

"No," she said without hesitation, and then guzzled her brew.

"Okay, so then who would you like to have sign this?"

"Well, I was kinda hoping I could."

"Well, yes, you will, but you also need somebody who is going to collect the money. It's called a life insurance policy to ensure that your friends and loved ones are confiscated in exchange for the loss and/or termination of your life."

"I understand that. But, let me ask you something: if *I* were to terminate *my* life, the money will still be available, right?"

"Suicide isn't paid out of the policy until two years after it's been in force. Why, is that something you are planning to commit?"

"That's something that's none of your business."

"Okay. But, should you pass away and are unable to collect the money – *because you're dead* – who would you like to receive it?"

Jade set her beer down, as she became frustrated. "Listen, buddy, another insurance broker said that I could fill out a policy with no questions asked," she exclaimed, and then extended her hand. "Just give me the form and show me where the dotted line is."

Ed sighed and handed his stubborn client the

application, "Here you go. But, it's not valid unless you get a beneficiary. That's the catch." Jade paused, and then let out a heavy sigh, as Ed noticed something interesting on her coffee table. It was a dusty, framed photo of a distinguished man in his early fifties. "What about this guy?" he asked her. "Would you like to make *him* the beneficiary?"

Jade turned to the photograph and suddenly became uncomfortable. She sighed, and then purposely knocked the photograph upside-down. "I've gotta go to work now," she told him. "So, if you don't mind..." She escorted Ed out of the house.

"Okay," he said, "well, thank you for your time. I must say –" Before he could complete his sentence, Jade closed the door in his face. "It's been a pleasure," he concluded, silently, and then headed back to the office.

CHAPTER 4:
MYSTERIOUS LEE

Obligated by his word, Ed joined Gary for lunch that afternoon at their usual place – an Italian restaurant and pizzeria called Savini's. He spotted Gary sitting at a table, browsing through a copy of the Arkanville Press – the village's free-based newspaper. He sat down, next to his colleague, "So, where's *Mysterious Lee*?"

"He's *mysteriously* late," Gary chuckled.

"How was your 10 o'clock?"

"Let's just say: I can't sell life insurance to an 89-year-old diabetic with one kidney and an iron lung. How was *your* appointment?"

"Let's just say: I can't sell life insurance to a

weird 27-year-old Goth woman with a fake suicide in mind."

"She actually tried to commit fraud?"

"Right in front of my face."

"No shit. So, are you going to report her?"

"Probably not. Let the next poor sap catch her."

"So, was she hot?" Gary asked him, enthusiastically. But, Ed gave him a look; he felt uncomfortable about the question. "What?" Gary asked, innocently. "It's a simple question."

"Gary, you know I couldn't possibly like her." He indicated his wedding band. "Besides, even if I were free and single she wouldn't be my type."

"Young and gorgeous?"

"Young and creepy."

On that note, a scraggly 30-something man with tinted eyeglasses sat across from them. He wore blue jeans, combat boots and a dark brown corduroy sports jacket over a black rock t-shirt. He removed his gray canvas shoulder bag and set it on the floor, next to his chair. Before acknowledging the guys, he spoke to the waitress: "Vodka and cranberry, hold the vodka." He felt the bewildered eyeballs of his company. So, he took the liberty to explain: "I try never to drink alcohol during the day. I tend to fall asleep too early and miss work when I do. Missing a whole evening's work makes me cranky. So, how are you fellas doing? Did you get my email, Gary?"

"I did, Lee. Thanks for the link, I really enjoyed

your website."

"Sweet," Lee grinned.

"So," Gary said to Lee, who had then graciously received – and sipped – his vodka and cranberry with no vodka. "This is the friend I was telling you about."

"Ed Talbot," he presumed.

"The one and only," Ed replied, sarcastically, and then they shook hands.

"So, you're the dude who saw those apparitions when you were four."

"Allegedly," Ed added.

"That's not uncommon. Babies and young children are actually susceptible to seeing ghosts – the ghosts know this, and therefore haunt the shit out of kids when they're alone. When I was a toddler I saw five faces in the dark, beside my bed. I screamed and cried until my mother heard me and switched the light on. The faces vanished, but my entire body was covered in hives. And, when I was a teenager – this is rare, but not completely uncommon – a man appeared in my bedroom and wiggled my nose. I thought it was my father. But, when I turned on the light nobody was there. I also woke up to my radio blaring on its own one night. Creepy shit."

Ed and Gary were in awe by Lee's weird – yet interesting rant.

"So, you see ghosts," Ed confirmed.

"Yes and no. As I got older I couldn't see them with the naked eye anymore. So, I moved out of the city a few months ago and setup base here. I took half that money that I used to put toward rent in my old rip off studio apartment and purchased infrared machines, radar – basically anything that I could use to document phantoms."

"Why Arkanville?" Ed asked with genuine curiosity.

"Excellent question, Ed. Because out of every city, town and village in New York, Arkanville is exposed to the most psychokinetic energy."

"Psychokinetic...?"

"In other words, Ed, Arkanville is contaminated with a colossal amount of supernatural shit."

"Why is that?"

"Either something extraordinary happened here *a long time ago* or something extraordinary *is going to happen real soon.*"

"Holy shit," Gary uttered.

"Well," Lee said, "if you want my opinion: I don't believe there's anything *holy* about it." He spotted a headline in Gary's Arkanville Press titled: THE MAD SCIENTIST – PROFESSOR VIKTOR DRODZ IS RELEASED FROM THE CROMWELL MENTAL INSTITUTION AFTER 24-YEARS. "Take this guy, for instance; this Professor Viktor Drodz. He was kept in a mental institution for several years, because, *supposedly,* his former students at the University reported his abrupt, abnormal behavior."

"He looks familiar," Ed suspected, as he stared at

the photographs of the corrupt professor.

Lee carried on: "Drodz spooked everyone when he began to blather about some experiment to reanimate dead tissue. He changed his curriculum from Biology to some kind of metaphysical necrology."

"It says here," Gary examined the article, "that he was working on finding a cure for death."

"Yeah," Lee replied. "You see: when Viktor Drodz was about thirteen-years-old, he and his family immigrated from Romania. They wanted the American dream, but what they got was an American nightmare. They lived in a penniless neighborhood and one night, when Viktor and his younger brother, Pavel, were out at the movies, a gang of punk teenagers invaded their home. They were robbed clean, with the parents left for dead – their throats slit."

"Damn," Gary chuckled, "you're like word-for-word with this article; you would think you wrote it."

"I did."

Gary was surprised, but disregarded his doubt when he finally read the fine print. "No shit."

"My cousin Emma used to work for Drodz's psychiatrist; *Dr. Praetor* – I wrote a paragraph on that asshole too. Yeah, just before she quit, Emma told me *all* about this Drodz dude. You know: he supposedly married, impregnated and murdered his college girlfriend too. But, when that went to trial in 1984, his lawyer had him plead insanity and then they took his kid away."

"That's messed up," Gary said.

"That's not even the half of it," Lee told him. "The asshole editor took out my paragraph about how Drodz believed he was in league with Lucifer – that's actually the part that made me so interested in this guy."

"You believe in the Devil?" Ed asked, affably.

"Well, not as my lord and savior, but yes. I do. If there are ghosts, there are angels – and if there are angels, there are demons."

"Ed is a bit skeptical, Lee. You'll have to excuse him."

"Well," Ed interjected, "let's just say that I'm the type of guy who has to see it to believe it."

"But, you did see it, dude," Lee told him. "When you were four."

"I'm pretty sure it was a night terror."

"In the middle of the day?" Gary asked, trying not to laugh.

"Okay," Ed chuckled, "it was a 'day terror!'"

At that point, Lee was the only one with a serious face. He drank his cranberry juice and then uttered, "Denial."

* * *

On his way back to the office, Ed began to feel a little impetuous. He thought it would be nice to visit his wife and surprise her with flowers. In spite of all the commotion in their daily lives, he thought that by implementing such a gesture would help revive their intimacy - which had actually been lacking for quite awhile. So, he picked up a dozen roses at a gas station, and then drove to her office building. He approached the cheerful receptionist and greeted her with a grin.

"Why, hello, Mr. Talbot," she smiled. "Are those for me?"

"Sorry, Dina, not today," he joked.

They laughed, but Dina was surprised. "Oh, really? You have another wife in this office that I don't know about?"

"I don't follow."

"You do know that Lena called in sick today, don't you? You do live with her, right?"

"Sick?"

"She was out yesterday too. Don't tell me you're one of those husbands who doesn't even pay attention to his wife."

Ed was at a complete loss. "I'll see ya," he said, stunned, and then headed for the exit. But, before he stepped out, something occurred to him. "Dina," he began to ask, as he walked back to her. "You didn't, by any chance, text my wife this morning, did you?"

"I don't believe in text-messaging."

"So, that's a *no*?" he assumed, and then walked out of the building with neurotic thoughts.

He threw the roses, in frustration, and then returned to his car. But, before he drove off, he attempted to contact Lena on his cell phone. He tried her cell and got her voicemail. He tried the house and got the answering machine. It was a shady situation. He even attempted to text-message her: *"Where are you?"* But, there was no response. Wherever she was, she certainly didn't want to be disturbed.

CHAPTER 5:
THE MAD SCIENTIST

Returning to Coolidge Avenue was not as easy as Professor Viktor Drodz had hoped. The site of his boarded
up, uninhabited house was enough to make him miss
the comfort of his padded cell. But, the memories
within are what affected him the most.

After he had broke the 'no trespassing' tape –
which surrounded his property – he pried his front
door open with a crowbar that Dr. Praetor provided
him with after his discharge. He even purchased a
brand new sedan for Drodz, which contained a box of
light bulbs and flashlights in the trunk, for when he
broke inside the house.

Fortunately, it was the mid-afternoon and his neighbors were away at work.

When the door busted open, the sunlight illuminated the living room. Everything was caked in dust and engulfed with spider webs.

He hesitated at the threshold when he caught sight of his framed wedding photo. The sight of his late wife broke his heart and his eyes flooded with impending tears.

Slowly and unsteadily, he followed the sunbeams into the house and lifted the photo. He wiped the dust off with his bare hands and then experienced a minor breakdown. The pain escalated. His heartbreak suddenly transformed into fury, and then he threw the photograph across the room. It shattered into pieces when it reached a wall in the shadows.

It took Drodz a moment to regain his natural calm and rational behavior.

He used one of his flashlights to find all of the lamps in the living room and replaced their bulbs.

When he secured himself in his home, he removed the area rug below his feet and opened a hidden door in the floor. He descended a steep wooden staircase, which led to his special basement.

Once illuminated, Drodz finally felt at home in his laboratory. All of his books on biology, neurology, chemistry and the occult – you name it – were scattered everywhere. On his desk, he found his personal journal, which contained the secrets to reanimate the dead.

Across from his desk stood his operating table, which was occupied with something beneath a filthy sheet.

Drodz was surprised, as he had almost forgotten what he had worked on before his imprisonment.

He approached the operating table and then hesitated before he could remove the sheet. But, his curiosity dominated his fear and he swiftly removed the sheet, revealing a rotted corpse of a male. It was more skeletal than Drodz remembered.

It was strapped to the table, but it gripped Drodz's arm unexpectedly and startled him.

"Why?" asked the corpse, hoarsely. It was his brother.

Drodz was not frightened. He was actually professional about this matter. "I was taken away, Pavel."

"You left me here to rot."

"I tried to save you. I explained everything to you. I had your consent at the hospital. Don't you remember?"

"I've been strapped to this table of yours for two decades, wondering when you would come back to finish me."

"I apologize."

"Now I am useless... I need you to complete me, Viktor."

"I will," Drodz said, as he released his dead brother from the restraining straps. "I may have something that could regenerate your tissue."

"No," Pavel exclaimed, as he sat up and wrapped his bony hand around Drodz's neck. "Complete my death."

"You're already dead," Drodz reminded him, as he attempted to pull his brother's hand off; and then he inadvertently snapped off his decomposed fingers in the process.

"If you won't, then I'll do it myself," Pavel said, as he climbed off the table and – like a toddler walking for the first time – staggered over to a concrete block and began to bash his bones from toe to head.

"No!" Drodz yelled, and then hurried over to Pavel.

"Don't try to stop me! You should burn in Hell for what you did!" he shouted, and then he finally smashed his skull into dust before Drodz could save what was left of him.

"Pity," said a sophisticated voice, accompanied by his clacking hooves.

Drodz turned to see his horn headed master, fully clad with an intimidating black overcoat, which covered his arrow-pointed tail. This, of course, was Lucifer.

"You let him suffer," Drodz accused the dark lord.

"I did no such thing, Viktor. The moment you traded his soul, for the knowledge that you so desperately require, Pavel's remains were exclusively in your custody. Have you forgotten that flesh means nothing to me? It's what's on the inside that matters."

"Is he alright?" Drodz asked, referring to his brother's captive soul.

"That's classified. You know that."

Drodz began to sweep up Pavel's dust particles and then turned to Lucifer, "Look: I know why you're here and I'm going to have to be honest with you; I will need time to catch up."

Lucifer clutched his protégé by the neck and lifted him up against the nearest wall. "You forget your place, Professor. The deal expires when you die. Do you want to die tonight?" Drodz replied with a nod, and then Lucifer retracted his grip. "You will proceed with your experiments, as planned. There is a young man in this village scheduled to cross on October 30th. You have till then to 'get settled.' When you achieve your part of the deal, I will return for his essence – *you know the ritual.*"

"Yes."

"It's good to have you back, Viktor," Lucifer grinned, diabolically, and then he finally vanished into black smoke.

* * *

For the very first time, Drodz visited his wife's grave. She was buried on a hill at Matheson Cemetery – Arkanville's only graveyard. The gothic cathedral where he and Keira were married stood majestically on the same property – and was in clear view – but it had been deserted for some time.

Despite the structure's hideous fate, he still thought that the view beyond the cathedral was as beautiful as it was decades ago. It was a cliff that offered an awe-inspiring view of the Long Island Sound, which happened to be the backdrop of their wedding photo.

The moonlight that reflected off the water captivated Drodz's vision until black clouds encompassed the sky. When the moonlight faded away, he had no choice but to continue to stare down at his wife's tombstone. "I made a mistake, Keira," he admitted out loud. "And, I know that I cannot fix what I've already done." He began to choke up, but held it together. "I miss you... so much."

The sky began to rumble with thunder, followed by a flash of lightning, and then finally... *rain.*

CHAPTER 6: SUSPICION

Ed returned home from work preoccupied – he appeared worried and was drenched from the pouring rain. When he set down his wet briefcase and hung up his soaked coat, he noticed Crystal setting the table in the dining room. Normally, Ed would smile at the sight of his daughter helping her mother with dinner, but not this time.

For a short while, Ed had been ignoring Lena's inconsistent behavior. It reminded him of 'the good old days' when she spent most of her time out of the house, on her own.

He couldn't help to notice how perfectly healthy

she appeared, preparing lasagna in the kitchen. She was actually quite chipper.

"Hey, Dad," Crystal greeted.

Ed snapped out of his 'world of terrible thoughts' and exchanged the greeting, "Hi, sweetheart."

But, Crystal sensed that something was amiss, "Are you okay, Dad? You look... nervous or something."

"Yeah, I'm fine, pumpkin."

"Hi, honey," Lena yelled from the kitchen. "I hope you're hungry."

"I was born hungry," he joked, and then smirked when he noticed his daughter chuckle.

"I poured you a soda," Crystal told him, as Ed followed her into the dining room to sit down.

"Thank you, but I think I'm in a beer mood tonight."

"Beer with dinner?"

"Yeah, why not?"

Crystal and Lena crossed paths at the kitchen threshold when Lena entered to place the tray of lasagna on the table. Just as soon as her hands were free, she planted a 'hello kiss' on her husband's cheek and then asked how his day was.

"Great," he told her. "How was yours?" He knew this was his opportunity to confirm what he dreadfully anticipated.

"Ah, pretty good," she said, as she began to

stretch. "Busy, as always."

Ed knew that she was full of shit; especially when she rubbed her eyes and threw in a yawn while answering – that was always her tell. "Tired?" he asked anyway.

"Yeah, I had so much to do today. You have no idea."

"Really…" he doubted, and then he changed his demeanor when Crystal returned with his beer and joined them at the table. "Ah, you're a lifesaver," he smiled and then immediately took a well-earned swig.

Lena found it odd that her husband chose an alcoholic beverage with dinner. In all of their years together, she had never seen him combine a beer with a meal before. But, she let it slide and then sat down to serve everyone the lasagna. She then bowed her head, as if to pray.

"So, kiddo," Ed said to Crystal, "how did you sleep last night? Were you and Owen comfortable?"

Lena quietly gave Ed an 'are you fucking kidding me?' stare. But, he had his conversation with Crystal anyway.

"Yeah," Crystal began, "I'm really sorry about that, Dad. Owen and I were so beat."

"From watching the horror marathon."

"There were like ten movies in a row."

"That's alright, Crystal. But, the next time you think that might happen just go to your bedroom and leave Owen in the living room. And, keep your door locked."

Crystal was pleased that her father didn't give her a hard time. But, Lena, on the other hand, was still giving Ed that stare.

"What?" Ed asked his wife, with an annoyed tone.

"We have to pray before the food gets cold."

Without any hesitation, Ed simply replied: "No we don't." This was also something very unfamiliar to his family.

"Excuse me?" Lena exclaimed. "Since when don't you want to say a prayer before we eat?"

"I don't want to talk about it," Ed answered. But, the truth of the matter was that Ed wasn't religious. His views on the subject opposed those who were followers – like his wife. It's not that Ed didn't believe in God and Heaven; he just believed that man was given a brain to use it and not ignore the endless possibilities and proven facts before us. The act of prayer made him feel like a hypocrite and his anger toward his deceitful wife compelled him to be a little selfish for a change. He refused to pray with his wife that evening, so he dug into his dinner. "Mmm," he grunted, "this is excellent!"

Lena snapped, "You're an asshole," and then she escaped to their bedroom without touching her plate.

Crystal lost her appetite, as well. But, she was very concerned and became nervous. "Dad, why are you acting like this?"

Ed sighed, and then spoke tenderly, "It's complicated."

"Did Mom do something?" she asked, as upsetting as that notion was for her.

He wanted to say "yes," but he hesitated and decided not to say anything at all. He reached into his wallet and then handed his daughter a couple of twenty-dollar bills. "Here," he said. "Why don't you and Owen go to a movie and grab something to eat."

"What's the catch?"

"The catch is that I upset your mother and now I want to apologize."

"You mean: *uninhibitedly*."

"Yeah," he smiled, "what you said." She smirked, and then he told her to be careful in the terrible weather – and *with Owen*, whom he could never trust.

* * *

Long after Crystal was gone, Ed visited Lena in their bedroom. She had been sobbing quietly on the bed for a while. "Hey," he said to her, calmly – yet callously. He wasn't allowing himself to give in to her tricks anymore.

"Don't speak to me," she said, adamantly.

"Fine," he replied, as he climbed into bed. "But, at least let me apologize. I didn't want you to skip dinner."

She responded with a loud, nasally sigh and then blew her nose. Apparently, her tears were aggravating her sinuses.

"Can I ask you something?"

She did the sigh again, and then asked, "What?"

"Why didn't you tell me that you didn't go to work today?"

"What do you mean?"

"I stopped by the office this afternoon and Dina told me that you called in sick."

"Oh, yeah," she suddenly recalled, "I had cramps. You know."

"I see," he alleged with uncertainty. "But, didn't you just have your period over a week ago?"

She began to act agitated, "Yeah, babe, sometimes it's early, okay?"

"Not that early."

She sighed – almost roared this time – but was able to maintain her composure. "I don't expect you to understand. You're not a woman."

Ed admired how his wife always managed to stay on her toes, whenever she found herself in a position to lie. It was as if she had a collection of excuses prepared in her head, ready to be used at any moment. This was the only thing that Ed ever resented about his marriage – Lena's lack of significant morals.

And, on that note, they fell asleep to the awkward silence that stood between them.

CHAPTER 7:
SHATTERED

Once again, Ed awoke to the sound of his 7:00AM alarm. And, once again, he suffered from the same nightmare – but, that was the least of his concern. He became more interested in his wife's mysterious absence. It was very inconsistent of her – and suspicious. She was always the last one out of bed and this new adjustment disturbed Ed.

He quickly threw on an outfit and then ran into Crystal in the hall. "Hey, kiddo," he said to her, "did you see your mother?"

"I think she just left," she answered, groggily, and then disappeared into the bathroom.

* * *

Lena had stepped out of the house before Ed could notice – and she was exceptionally dolled up. She was clearly out to impress someone. At least, that's what Ed thought when he caught sight of her driving away from the house.

As Ed's abrupt fury became possessed with adrenaline, he immediately grabbed his keys and unleashed one of his slick motorcycles from the two-door garage. He managed to reach Lena's car relatively quick, but also made a conscious effort to keep a considerable distance.

It was only a short moment before she made a turn onto Evergreen Drive – only six blocks away from their home on Warwick Road.

Ed stopped his bike just as soon as Lena pulled up to an unrecognizable high-class residence. When he saw her reach the front door, he watched a well-mannered, sophisticated man in his mid-forties give her an affectionate greeting. Ed felt his heart sink into his stomach. It took him a while to rebuild his rationale but, when he finally did, he rode away.

* * *

Ed visited Gary at the office – *he was a nervous wreck*. He explained everything to his friend, quietly and confidentially. "It's William Praetor," he told Gary, sternly.

"William Praetor?" The name sounded familiar

to Gary, but it took him a moment to recall who he actually was.

"Yes. Dr. William Praetor. The guy in the paper! The psychiatrist that released Drodz."

"Why?"

"How the hell should I know?" Ed howled.

"How long do you think it's been going on?"

"Probably since September. That's when she started getting random text-messages – which, she always said were from her friend, Dina. But, that was bullshit. The woman doesn't even like to text! I'm furious, Gary. I don't know what I'm gonna do! You know: if this were the other way around, she'd chop off my dick and feed it to the sharks – *which she so elegantly stated to me once.*"

Despite Gary's sudden urge to make a joke, he focused on the nature of Ed's dilemma. "Does Crystal know?" he asked, gently.

Gary's question was enough to initiate Ed's impulsive exit. He left work, unannounced, and then rode his bike back home.

* * *

Before Ed returned to his residence, he remembered that Crystal had work that day. So, he altered his course and visited her job - a coffeehouse on Main Street. Unfortunately, Ed learned that she had only worked a half-day and had just left with her boyfriend. On that note, Ed ordered himself a large cup of black coffee and returned to his vacant house.

He spent the rest of the afternoon in the living room, sipping on his 24oz coffee, with his legs elevated on his recliner. He kept the shades down and the lights dim, as he listened to some Beethoven and tried to re-lax. But, no matter what he did, he could not escape his thoughts.

The solitude actually allowed him to think deeper. He began to realize things that he always chose to ignore, like the loss of his father, who had recently passed away from heart disease. He also worried about his poor mother spending her residual time in the sun-shine state. But, he eventually returned to the issue at hand: *the inevitable final days of his marriage*.

Even if Lena would eventually come to her senses, put a stop to Dr. Praetor and apologize to Ed, he wouldn't give her the satisfaction. Betrayal leaves a scar and he wouldn't be able to look at his wife the same way ever again. Reconciling was definitely out of the question.

When Ed realized that he was down to a half cup of coffee, he took a bottle of Irish whiskey and topped it off.

And, as the daylight began to fade away, so did Ed. His Irish coffee delivered a successful buzz, but it had also put him straight to sleep. Evidently, the caf-feine had very little affect on him.

* * *

Sometime between the hour of 6PM and 7PM, Ed awoke to the sound of Lena entering the house – which he did not prepare himself for. Buzzed or not, he became overwhelmed with several variations of emotion – they all struck him simultaneously.

He wanted to yell.

He wanted to weep.

He wanted to punch her in the head.

But, he did none of those things. Instead, he took his fury and his arrogance and hopped off his chair to chase his wife down the hall. He startled her just before she could enter the bedroom.

"Holy shit, Ed!" she yelled. "What's the matter with you?"

"You, Lena. You."

"What?" she asked him, without even realizing his true implication. She still thought that she was getting away with murder, so she played dumb.

Ed, of course, was not fooled. "Work late?" he asked, sarcastically.

"Oh, yeah," she lied. "What a day; let me tell you…" She honestly thought that she could get off the hook with her response, and then attempted to enter the bedroom.

But, Ed wasn't going to let her get away with it. "Bullshit!" he barked, and then she froze to peer over her shoulder.

She spun around to face him again. "What did you say?" she asked, nervously. Lena finally began to suspect that her husband wasn't so dumb anymore.

"You heard me," he told her, as he began to advance her. "Do you honestly think that I can't see past your lies, Lena? Do you really think that you could get away with them?"

"Edward, you're frightening me!" she cried.

"I know what you did, honeybunch," he said, heatedly. "I know that you've been spending your afternoons fucking that psychiatrist."

Lena was stunned and extremely surprised that Ed caught her, after all that time she had been messing behind his back – we're talking months. "Edward, I –"

"You destroyed this marriage, Lena," Ed stated. "How could you do this to me? How could you do this to my daughter?"

"*Our* daughter," she cried.

"Oh, we'll just see about that; you didn't even raise her! You know why? Because you're a selfish bitch!"

Lena became too choked up to argue. The pressure of Ed's attack was emotionally overwhelming. She fled from the house, hysterically, and left Ed alone with his frenzy.

CHAPTER 8:
WEAR AND TEAR

Dr. William Praetor had become a very wealthy psychiatrist, but never had enough time to settle down. It wasn't until the end of August 2008 when he finally fell in love. He met Lena, while inquiring about legal advice for his estate and it was an unprecedented, vigorous connection. He made every effort to sweep her off her feet. He didn't even care that she wore a wedding band – and, neither did she, apparently.

Praetor and Lena had several afternoon dates since their first encounter. She used up all of her personal days to be with him. Now, she was using up her sick time. But, he was nothing but a lustful fixation to her and she could not resist him. If it wasn't for his classy personality and his rugged good looks, then it was certainly all about his fortune.

But, Praetor wasn't a total pompous, wine-guzzling schmuck. He also liked his beer and sports, which were exactly what he enjoyed before Lena returned to his house. He sprawled on his suede sofa, guzzled cold Belgian ale and began to watch a football game on television. But, he was surprised to see Lena again, after already spending the entire afternoon with her. He immediately noticed her anguish and welcomed her in. "What's the matter, baby," he asked, as she jumped into his warm embrace. "Is everything alright?"

"He knows, Will," she muttered.

"How?"

"I don't know. But, he figured it out and he knows it's you. *He knows who you are!*"

"Alright, just calm down. Have a seat; relax. Would you like a drink?"

"Something strong."

"You got it," he told her, and then poured her a glass of brandy. "I told you it was only a matter of time before he'd find out. Deception – although *effective* to a persuasive person – is impermanent. You should just divorce Ed and get it over with."

"I didn't come back here to hear your professional advice. I'm here because I need you."

"The advice is free, babe," he said, as he handed

her the brandy. "What do you want to do?"

She drank the drink in one shot. "Do you want the truth?"

"Sure."

"The truth is – as luck would have it – Ed is worth a lot more than I am."

"I don't follow."

"I'm in love with you, Will. I really am. But, the reason why this is so complicated for me is because I'm also very much in love with Ed's assets."

"Really? You do know that I make a respectable living..."

"No, I know. Trust me, I know. But, I've worked too hard and too long in that marriage, Will. I've earned my husband's money!"

"True, but if you divorce him you'll still receive a settlement."

"I only get *half*. It's nothing compared to what I'd get if I were still his spouse. His will states this – I should know; I drafted the damn thing. Even his life insurance policy would be useless to me."

"Well, then you should just amend the will."

"I can't. It's set in stone. It specifically states that everything goes to his *spouse*."

"Okay, so don't divorce him; just separate."

"That wouldn't fly. Ed hates me with a passion right now. If I don't divorce him, he will divorce me."

"Well, I guess that only leaves you with one option."

"Yeah, I know, I have to make the first move."

"That's not exactly what I'm suggesting, babe," he said, as he indicated his mounted collection of exotic daggers.

Lena hesitated before she imagined what Praetor was suggesting. *Eradication.* She was disturbed by it, "No! Absolutely not! No, William! That is *not* happening!"

"Then, you will be miserable for the rest of your life. Do you think you could live with that regret forever, Lena?"

"I may not love him. I may want his money. But, I will not, under any circumstances, murder my husband! Are you insane? Do you know what that could do to us? Police will be at our door every day until they finally figure it out. You said so yourself: *deception* is impermanent."

"It would look like an accident, Lena," he assured her. "I promise."

She was appalled by his sadistic lure. "What kind of psychiatrist are you?"

"I'm only a psychiatrist behind a desk. Right now, I am a man who wants to make the woman he loves happy."

Lena thought it through, "Everything will go to Crystal anyway. She'll take care of her mother."

"Yes, but when's that, another forty-years or so? By that time, you're not going to care about the vanity, glamour and materials anymore. You'll be blowing it all on doctor bills and medicine."

Lena's hopes were suddenly shot down. She felt compelled to think about it some more, only to realize that there was no other alternative. "In the event of his death I get everything – and, I mean *everything*."

Praetor smirked and raised his ale. "And, you *do* want *everything*, right?"

* * *

Ed couldn't find anything interesting to watch on television. He came across the continuous horror movie marathon, but he wasn't in the mood for it. So, he channel-surfed. It was around midnight and there was nothing else on except for infomercials.

He had been alone all night and was still hitting the bottle – this time: Irish whiskey on the rocks.

Crystal eventually snuck into the house, hoping that her father wouldn't catch her. She did her best to avoid facing him and, when Ed finally noticed her, she slipped into her bedroom and slammed the door.

Even buzzed, Ed sensed that his daughter was in some sort of trouble. He climbed off the recliner and approached Crystal's bedroom. "Crystal?" he asked, softly, and then he tapped on the door.

"Please, leave me alone, Dad," she sobbed, politely.

Ed was too disturbed by her dilemma. "What's wrong, pumpkin?" She ignored him, and then he assumed that Lena could've spoken to her. He knocked on the door until she finally opened it.

When she did, he saw that tears were pouring down her face. He also noticed that her left eye was bruised.

"What happened?" he exclaimed. But, Crystal had trouble explaining. Instead, she left the door open and sat on her bed, upset. Ed sat next to her. "What happened?" he asked again, sympathetically.

It wasn't easy for Crystal, but her comforting father was patient. Finally, she began to explain: "Owen," she uttered, and then she choked up before she could complete her sentence. It didn't matter; Ed was able to fill in the blanks. But, she attempted to continue anyway, "He, um..."

"He punched you, didn't he?" he asked, as he clenched his jaw.

Crystal began to bawl and she buried her face in her father's arms. "I kept telling him 'no,' but he wouldn't listen. I told him to stop, but he was forceful. And, then he hit me!" she cried.

At that point, Ed knew it was safe to assume what had happened. Without a doubt, Owen wanted his "needs" taken care of and Crystal had the will to reject him.

"Why would he do that?" she cried. "Why couldn't he just respect my feelings?"

"Pumpkin," he said, gently – yet his adrenaline was pumping, "Sometimes people who we'd like to trust have a dark side. We just have to take our chances. And, that's what life is really about: taking chances and experiencing things..."

Crystal remained silent until she was finally able to calm herself down. "Is mom asleep?" she asked.

"Your mother's out, kiddo," he told her, and then attempted to change the subject by offering to get her an icepack for her eye.

The phone began to ring, as Ed retrieved an ice-pack from the freezer. He froze – *no pun intended* – and suspected that the caller could've either been Owen or Lena. He hesitated before answering.

The voice on the other end was Lena. "Are you calmer now?" she asked her husband.

"Not at all. What do you want?"

After her infamous sigh, she said, "Look: I just wanted to apologize, okay. I was a fool. What I did was immoral and hypocritical – I've realized that."

"What you did was irreversible. Our vows obviously meant nothing to you. What happened to 'in sickness and health' and 'until death do we part,' and all that shit? I mean, come on, Lena, you've coveted our neighbor's ass, for crying out loud!"

"I want to make it up to you," she said, entic- ingly.

"I don't think so."

"Maybe we should talk about this when you cool off."

"Maybe you should go fuck yourself, you dia- bolical bitch!" he barked, and then slammed the phone down. Unfortunately, he noticed Crystal staring at him from the kitchen threshold. He handed her the icepack, and then poured her a glass of juice before returning to the living room.

Crystal joined him, as he turned off the television with the remote. "So," she began to ask her father. "That was mom, wasn't it?" She took his silence as a 'yes.' "You're gonna get divorced, aren't you?"

Ed took a sip of whiskey before he answered. "If we continue to stay together it will become very uncomfortable and dysfunctional."

"It's already dysfunctional, dad!" she cried. "And, it will stay dysfunctional when you separate!"

"I didn't ask for this, Crystal, okay! It's your mother's doing, not mine!"

"What did she do? Tell me."

"You don't want to know, kiddo."

"I have a right to know!"

Ed disapproved her knowing, but he saw that Crystal was going to remain persistent about it. "Your mother's been cheating on me." He noticed that Crystal was about to have an emotional breakdown. "And, I'm sorry, pumpkin, but I'm through with her."

Her breakdown became overwhelming and she unexpectedly ran out of the house, hysterically crying.

"Crystal!" Ed shouted, as he attempted to chase after her. But, by the time he got outside, she was nowhere to be seen. "Crystal!" he cried again, but nothing.

* * *

Ed didn't care what time it was when he decided to visit the Murphy residence – it was only moments after his daughter ran off. He knew that this would probably be the last place Crystal would go, but it pleased him to stopover anyway.

He climbed up the brick doorsteps and rang the bell several times. Eventually, a very worn-out Owen opened the door. "Mr. Talbot," he said, in a daze. "What are you doing here?"

"Is Crystal here, by any chance?"

"No, she went home an hour ago."

"I see," he sighed, and then he had a new thought: "Are your parents awake?"

"It's one-thirty in the morning!"

"I guess I'll take that as a 'no,'" Ed retorted, and then he grabbed Owen by the head and slammed his face against the iron handrail. The kid's eyes flooded with tears and his nose began to gush blood. "Don't *EVER* touch my daughter again! Do you hear me, *fuck-head*?" Without another word, Ed proudly abandoned Owen and returned home.

Ah, sweet justice

CHAPTER 9:
A MERCILESS MORNING

After an early breakfast appointment with a new client, Ed returned home only to find his wife's car parked in the driveway. He wasn't too thrilled about that, but he also wasn't afraid to confront her.

He didn't see anyone inside the house – not even Crystal, who was still missing in action. He explored the rooms until he eventually discovered Lena in the bedroom. She was disturbingly extravagant in her lingerie and sprawled out on a bed of rose pedals. If they weren't having marital issues, Ed would've jumped her bones in a heartbeat. But, her natural beauty was too obscured by her wicked intentions. "What the hell is this?" he winced.

"I just wanted to apologize and make it up to you," she smiled.

But, Ed wasn't buying it. "My decision is final, Lena."

She remained confidently tantalizing, as she moved closer to him. "Now, that isn't very fair, Eddy. I know that we haven't been intimate with each other for a long, long time," she said, as she began to caress his crotch region. "I thought we could go back to the way it used to be. You know: *In here*."

Ed smacked her hand away. "Get out!" he commanded. "Right now!"

"Are you kidding me?"

Ed collected her outfit from the floor and then threw it at her.

"Ed, you're being unreasonable!"

"Sorry. I'm not into sloppy seconds, baby," he said, as he returned to the living room. "I'm calling the police, if you don't get your ass out of my house."

"It's our house!" she cried, while getting dressed.

"Yeah, well, we'll see about that," he mumbled, as he attempted to grab the cordless phone from the coffee table. But, an unwelcome guest intercepted it – it was Praetor. Ed promptly swung his fist and sent Praetor into the dining room.

Praetor's presence was an even greater disturbance for Ed. As he attempted to escape the house, Lena dashed out of the bedroom, armed with one of

Praetor's collectable daggers, and she double-locked the exit.

"What," Ed asked her, as he noticed the blade. "Are you gonna kill me now? Breaking my heart wasn't enough for ya?"

Lena was upset. She attempted to speak, but then she saw an enraged Praetor advance Ed from behind.

"It's best not to communicate right now," Praetor said, dourly. "It'll break the mood."

"What?" Ed shrieked.

"You do it," she told Praetor, as she handed him his dagger. "I can't bring myself to it."

"The blade was just to scare him, baby."

Ed knew that he was targeted for murder and, as Lena and Praetor bickered, he attempted to make a run for it. But, Praetor tackled him before he could get anywhere. "Not so fast!" he told Ed, as he kept him pinned to the floor. Fortunately, Ed was able to knee him in the groin and slip away.

The knife had fell, but Lena retrieved it once Ed attempted to unlock the front door. She pointed it at her husband's face and he had no choice but to remain still. "Why are you doing this to me?" Ed howled.

She actually shed a tear, and then apologized, "I'm sorry, baby."

"Fuck you!" he hollered, and then he fled the house before she could jab the dagger into his chest.

Praetor stormed after him.

"Where are you going?" she yelled.

"I told you: this is going to look like an accident," Praetor promised, as he observed Ed sprinting up the street. He hopped into his car and callously pursued him. He accelerated his vehicle until he was able to strike Ed severely.

Lena couldn't believe her eyes. She had to cover her mouth, as she gasped, and then she ran back inside the house, hysterical.

Praetor quickly shifted the car into park, and then stepped out to examine Ed's condition. "Oh, dear," Praetor said, cynically. "What happened? Oh, no. What a tragedy." He flipped Ed on his back and saw that he was barely conscious.

Ed attempted to speak, but he was paralyzed and suffering.

"Sweet dreams, bub, " Praetor said, before suffocating him with his bare hands. He witnessed Ed expire and then, with a convincing tone of concern, he alerted the absentminded neighborhood: "Somebody call an ambulance!"

* * *

Ed's obituary went something like this:

EDWARD MICHAEL TALBOT MURDERED AT 43; INSURANCE BROKER AND MOTORCYCLE ENTHUSIAST. He was born in Manhattan on October 6, 1965 and was killed on Long Island on October 30, 2008 by an unidentified careless driver, while crossing

Warwick Road in Arkanville, New York. He was a beloved husband, a compassionate father and a respectful friend to those who knew him.

A wake service will be held at the Romero Funeral Home, located at 660 Main Street, Arkanville, NY on October 31, 2008 at 7:00PM. His burial has been arranged for November 1, 2008 at 9:30AM in the Matheson Cemetery. May he rest in peace.

* * *

The news naturally devastated Ed's true loved ones.

When Crystal returned home from spending the night at her girlfriend's house – her co-worker, Mandy McKellen, from the coffeehouse – her mother told her the disturbing announcement. Of course, it was Lena's Machiavellian version.

Apparently, a drunk driver hit her father and a bystander witnessed the entire thing.

Poor Crystal suspected that her father could've been searching the streets for *her*. But, that idea only made the news much more severe. She cried for hours that day, in solitary.

* * *

Gary received the news from Lee, who had noticed the obituary at the Arkanville Press. Coincidentally, Lee had been keeping an eye on the death toll, in an effort to document what he called "The Ascension Effect," which is supposedly when the spirit detaches itself from a corpse before it travels to wherever it's meant to go. But, Gary was not interested in that – not when it came to the death of his best friend.

Lee eventually realized how insensitive he sounded, and then he took his buddy out for a drink – this time, he ordered vodka with his cranberry juice. Gary, on the other hand, consumed a massive amount of whiskey.

CHAPTER 10:
R.I.P.

There is a young man in this village scheduled to cross on October 30th.

Drodz made a conscious effort to remember the Devil's advice; it was his highest priority. And, with that in mind, he made an effort to study Ed's obituary in the Arkanville Press that Halloween morning.

He opened an inoperative furnace and removed three numbered syringe guns. Syringe #1 was a green fluid; #2 was a red fluid; and #3 was suspiciously empty.

According to his journal, each syringe represented a significant change in some kind of warped procedure:

Stage #1: Stabilization.

Stage #2: Reanimation.

Stage #3: Extraction.

He referred to the Stage #1 and #2 fluids as formulas. But, in reality, they were a concoction materialized by the Devil himself. However, Lucifer was only interested in the stage-3 syringe.

* * *

Drodz found it amusing to dress up in a costume that afternoon. He posed as a mortician and slipped into the local morgue, while the real professionals took their lunch break.

He located Ed's cadaver with no problem, and then removed the stage-1 syringe from his satchel. He jabbed the needle into Ed's forehead, and then injected the green fluid into the brain.

According to Drodz's records, the human brain is a computer, and his goal was to simply reboot it. The second syringe was designed for that very purpose. So, he released the red fluid into Ed's skull.

Based on his experience with his brother, Drodz knew that the formulas would eventually settle within 48-hours, which, according to his research, is the amount of time it takes for a soul to detach itself from a corpse – *the ascension effect*.

Finally, he removed the stage-3 syringe but, before he could use it, the real morticians returned to their post. He had no choice but to pack up and retreat.

* * *

Drodz raced his car down the narrow, wooded road that brought him to the morgue. But, before he could even reach a mile, an unfamiliar tunnel – which did not exist earlier – swallowed his vehicle.

He quickly shifted the car into park, when he realized that there was no light at the end of the tunnel – and, even worse, the entrance behind him had vanished. He was trapped in total darkness.

"I believe you owe me something," said Lucifer, as he manifested from the shadows ahead.

Drodz stepped out of his car and tensely stood before his ominous benefactor. "I never reached stage-3."

In a blink of an eye, Lucifer revealed his true, monstrous form. He was a ten-foot winged creature with black eyes and a body proportioned like a dragon. He attacked his disciple and shackled him with his elongated tail. And, then he spoke in his thunderous, menacing voice: "I could tear you to shreds in a single heartbeat." But, he didn't. Instead, he morphed back into his original facade and released Drodz from his grasp. "But," he continued in his sophisticated voice, "I'm gonna give you a break, Viktor; just this once. I can't blame you for being out of practice."

Drodz was still petrified from experiencing the Devil's ferocity, but he held his dignity. "I can go back."

"You have till midnight," Lucifer ordered, and then he leaned in closer to his face, and said, "I want that soul." Without another word, Lucifer returned to the shadows, and then evaporated with the surrounding darkness.

Drodz found himself back on that wooded road again.

* * *

Ed's wake was held at the Romero Funeral Home. Relatives and friends were in attendance. Gary had his entire office there, as well. Lee even made an appearance. But, even more interesting, *so did Drodz.*

Drodz was incognito – a wig and a pair of bold eyeglasses. He also wore a long raincoat, which, without a doubt, contained the stage-3 syringe in one of the pockets.

"Nice costume," Lee surprised Drodz, as he snuck up behind him.

"Pardon?" Drodz asked, innocently.

"What, you think nobody would recognize you in that get up? I know who you are. What the hell are you doing at Ed Talbot's wake?"

"I'm afraid you've lost me, my friend."

"You're professor Drodz."

"I'm James Finnegan, Edward's uncle. And, you?"

"Never mind," Lee said, disappointedly, and

then he found Gary.

"Hey," Gary greeted him.

But, Lee was preoccupied. "Remember that crazed scientist that I told you about the other day?"

"You mean the one you wrote the article about? The Romanian guy?"

"Yeah. Drodz. I think he's here."

"What? You've gotta be kidding me. What on earth would he be doing at Ed's wake?"

"Well, isn't it obvious? He probably wants to bring Ed back."

"You're weird, dude."

"And, you're a crotch-sniffing ho-bag. Nobody's perfect."

"Touché. Alright, where is he?"

Lee attempted to point Drodz out, but he lost him in the crowd. "Shit, he was just over there."

"Well, if you see him pulling any crap, let me know; I'll kick his ass."

"Wait a minute," Lee had an epiphany, "wouldn't you rather see if he can actually do what they say he can do?"

"What, play God? I don't think so."

On the other side of the room, Crystal was sitting beside her mother. Between the two of them, she was the only one who produced genuine tears.

"Are you alright, sweetie?" Lena asked. "You haven't said a word all day."

"I have nothing to say, Mom," she answered,

glumly.

Lena sighed, "Did you tell Owen?" Crystal shook her head 'no.' "Why not?"

"Mom, please, not right now!" Evidently, Crystal was not in the mood to chat or have a discussion about her ex-boyfriend.

When Lena turned her head away, aggravated by her daughter's attitude, she noticed Drodz standing in line to pay his respects. She eventually talked herself into approaching him and then introduced herself.

Drodz politely acknowledged her, "Hello, Mrs. Talbot. I am Kurtwood Stark; your husband and I were old friends." He intentionally made up another fake name to avoid any risk with Ed's wife.

"Nice to meet you. Thank you so much for coming, it means a lot. But, I have to admit your name doesn't ring a bell."

"Well, Edward and I were acquainted a long time ago. We used to work together."

"Oh, that's nice."

When it finally became Drodz's turn to approach the casket, he excused himself and Lena gave him privacy.

He kneeled before Ed's corpse and gestured the act of prayer, while he reached into one of his pockets. He discretely removed the stage-3 syringe gun, jabbed it into Ed's temple and then extracted a florescent blue haze. When finished, he quickly pocketed the syringe and then quietly recited a mystifying chant: "Karabok, shantarok, valadok." He stood up and took a moment of silence. "Until we meet again," he said, under his breath, and then left the building stealthily.

However, Lee was sharp enough to notice Drodz's silent escape. He spotted him from across the room, and then attempted to pursue him, without warning Gary – who, at that point, was summoned to the front of the room to perform the eulogy.

"Good evening," Gary said to the crowd. "For those of you who don't know me, my name is Gary Walker; I've worked with Ed for quite a number of years." He took a deep breath, and then he referred to his written speech. "When I was a kid," he recited, "my memory of these things were of the elderly having lived their lives and saying goodbye. My adult life experiences have not been the same. I have seen too many people leave us before their time. I have learned that life is a collection of memories that are shared, that are given and that are received. All we have now are the memories we shared for his short life, but these are the ones that we must hold and cherish for the rest of our days. Ed was a great man. He loved his job, he loved his clients and, more importantly, he loved his family – especially his daughter, Crystal. I will always remember Ed as my best friend and, from this day forth, we must replace the suffering of his loss with the joy of his life." He began to choke up, and then pocketed his heartfelt speech. "Thank you."

Everybody was touched and proudly applauded

Gary, as he returned to his seat. But, Lena stopped him to give him a huge hug. "Thank you for that, Gary," she told him. But, Gary didn't appreciate her gratitude at all. He kept silent and gave her the cold shoulder.

CHAPTER 11:
ALL HALLOW'S EVE

When Lee drove his car, in pursuit of Drodz, he was surprised to see all of the holiday paraphernalia – shaving cream, silly string, toilet paper and eggshells were everywhere. Even the smell of colored hairspray contaminated the air. He couldn't recall a Halloween turnout like this since he was a young boy in the 1980s. Apparently, between the daylight savings extension and it being a Friday night, Arkanville faced a tremendous response. By dark, the village was already swarming with costumed teenagers.

Lee kept his distance, and then parked near a toilet-papered tree when Drodz turned down Coolidge

Avenue. He observed Drodz avoiding the trick-or-treaters on his way to his house. And, after he snubbed all the kids, he hurried inside.

That was Lee's cue to step out of his car and trespass on Drodz's property. He saw that the windows were still boarded up, so he gave the front door a shot – it was surprisingly unlocked.

He took extra precaution when he entered the house; however, Drodz was nowhere to be found. But, Lee's investigating habits tempted his need to explore.

In the midst of his intrusive search, he stumbled upon a desk and quietly began to rummage through the drawers. He eventually came across a book on demonology, a few *downgraded* letters, and then an old wallet-sized photo of Drodz's wife and daughter. But, as he continued to uncover the contents of the desk, he came to the conclusion that it belonged to Keira Drodz.

He knew that Viktor Drodz was a deranged scientist, but this was the desk of a witch. The discovery of Keira's diary confirmed his notion. It was a leather-bound book that contained, not only her personal thoughts, but also an abundance of incantations and bizarre ritualistic practices. Lee could not resist this treasure, so he swiped it and suddenly considered the idea of evading the troubling residence.

As Lee attempted to make his exit, he was startled by the sound of obnoxious knocking. He halted and anticipated Drodz to appear, *but he didn't*. So, Lee took the liberty of opening the door and saw a group of decked out teens that shouted, "TRICK OR TREAT!"

"Holy shit!" Lee exclaimed, startled, and then he hesitated. "This isn't my house. Try the next one, guys."

He left the house, and abandoned the disappointed trick-or-treaters. They watched him return to his car, and then one of them shouted, "Asshole!" But, that didn't insult Lee at all. He just got into his car, started her up and drove away. But, little did he know that his bumper now occupied the words: "I HAVE A HALLOW WEENIE" spray-painted on it.

* * *

Ed's corpse was still in the custody of the Romero Funeral Home and was scheduled for a brief service the next morning, prior to his transport to Matheson Cemetery. But, Ed had rejected his coffin that evening and incoherently declined his own funeral by escaping the building.

As he slipped through the one-way exit, his coffin had miraculously closed itself, which would later deceive his mourners – but that was neither here nor there.

Despite the fact that he was a walking dead man, his actions were preset – as if he was under some kind of hypnotic spell. In a manner of speaking, Ed sleepwalked out of the funeral home and into the heart of the festivities.

Conveniently, all of the trick-or-treaters accepted

Ed as a man dressed as a zombie. He even received compliments for the duration of his involuntary stroll.

"Nice costume!" said a young, latex werewolf.

"Hey, great make-up!" said a rubber alien.

"Where's your candy bag?" asked a petite she-devil.

But, Ed's oblivion overrode his potential to respond. He didn't even react to a car that virtually clipped him, when he turned onto Coolidge Avenue.

When he finally reached his unforeseen destination – *Drodz's vandalized home* – the eccentric professor greeted him at the front door. "Welcome, Mr. Talbot," he grinned. "I've been expecting you."

CHAPTER 12:
DEATH'S A BITCH

It was twenty-three minutes before the stroke of midnight when Drodz conducted a few adjustments to Ed's reanimated carcass. Ed was shackled to the table that once occupied Pavel Drodz and was clamped with wires, which delivered electric currents from a generator. Drodz referred to this procedure as a revitalization technique, which was actually the icing on the cake. The end result was likely to rejuvenate Ed's vigilance and character.

On his journey to consciousness, Ed witnessed his entire life repeat itself in a simultaneous blur. Subsequently, he soon realized that he was trapped in an unknown basement. "Am I in Hell?" he asked himself, lethargically, and without noticing the professor.

"You're on a detour," Drodz humored him.

But, Ed found nothing amusing about his state of affairs. As far as he knew, Dr. Praetor hit him with a car, and then his former patient kidnapped him. At least, that's how it appeared. "What did you do to me?" Ed asked. "Did they put you up to this?"

"What I did," Drodz began, as he detached the wires from Ed, "was salvage you, Mr. Talbot."

"Salvage me?" Ed asked, confused. "Why aren't I in a hospital?"

"You were. *Briefly.*"

"What do you mean? Why am I fastened to a workbench in your goddamn cellar?"

Drodz released Ed from the shackles, allowing him to sit upright. "You know who I am?" Drodz confirmed, inquisitively.

"You've had ten-minutes of fame in the '80s and you were the front headline in Monday's paper. Now, what the hell did you do to me, you sick bastard? Why am I here?"

"I'll get to that. But, I warn you: you will not like what I tell you."

"Try me."

"What's the last thing you remember?"

"What's with the questioning? I asked for an answer."

"With questions will come answers."

"You sound like a fucking fortune cookie."

"Mr. Talbot, please: what was the very last thing that happened to you, before you awoke in my lab?"

"I was running away from Lena – my former wife – and Praetor, her *soon-to-be-dead* admirer. I ran up my block, and then I remember getting hit by Praetor's car..." Ed found himself falling into a stupor, as he envisioned the sinister occurrence. "I fell on the ground... paralyzed."

"When you say the name Praetor, you do not mean *Dr. William Praetor*... Do you?"

"Small world, huh?"

Drodz was stunned, but tried to remain focused. "And, do you feel paralyzed now?" Drodz quizzed him.

"No," he replied, dumbfounded. "I don't feel anything. No pain. No heat. No cold." Ed became nervous and uneasy. He proceeded with his recollection, "Praetor kneeled over me and... and, he..."

"And, *he what*, Mr. Talbot?"

"He suffocated me," Ed complained; he was disturbed.

"*To death*, I might add," Drodz contributed, as he handed Ed a small mirror to prove his lack of breath.

"Oh my God!" Ed exclaimed, aghast. "I'm not breathing!"

"Nor do you have to."

Ed leaped off the table and panicked when he realized that he had no heartbeat or pulse. "I have no heart!" he shrieked.

"In a literal sense, that is correct."

"Am I...?" Ed didn't even want to say it: "Am I fucking dead?"

"I would use the term 'undead,' but that word is usually associated with vampires; which you are not."

"This is a nightmare. This can't be for real!"

"You should be thrilled, Mr. Talbot."

"Please don't call me Mr. Talbot; it makes me sound like an old man."

"You have an opportunity to prosper."

"So, everything they said – *about how you were looking to raise the dead* – all of that is true?"

"You are proof, Edward. This is scientific fact now, and you were chosen."

"Chosen by whom?" Ed asked, suspiciously.

But, before Drodz could answer him, they were interrupted by the sound of midnight. Every clock in the house went berserk, simultaneously.

"I'm getting the hell out of here," Ed said, flustered, and then he searched for an exit.

"I would have to advise against that, Edward. In fact, I forbid it right now."

"What, you think just because you gave me life you can order me around? You're not a god, professor." And, with that said, Ed found the stairs to the living room.

"No!" Drodz panicked, and then he desperately attempted to stop his *guest* before he slipped out the front door. But, he was too late. In Ed's favor, Drodz was constrained from exiting the house by an extraordinary blaze of lightning, accompanied with an abrupt wail of thunder. He almost fell backward, and down the basement stairs, but managed to hold himself up when he grabbed onto his wife's desk. When his vision quickly recovered from the blinding flash, he realized that Ed was long gone.

"Time is up," said Lucifer.

Drodz turned and saw the Devil sitting patiently on a gothic armchair. "He escaped," Drodz whimpered.

"Corpse or no corpse, you owe me that man's soul."

In disbelief, Drodz forced himself to unlock his safe, which was tritely embedded in the wall, behind a mystical painting.

"You put too much trust in your experiments," Lucifer said to Drodz, as he watched him remove a jar that contained the blue hazy substance. This, of course, was Ed's essence – *his soul.* "Perhaps," Lucifer continued, "you should keep them chained in your laboratory and refrain from removing the hypnotic hex."

"Because," Drodz began, as he handed Lucifer the jarred soul, "unlike you, I do not believe in eternal captivity."

"That's a shame," Lucifer said, as he graciously accepted the soul. "You've done well, Viktor."

Drodz was about to say something else, but he

had lost his train of thought when they were interrupted by another startling crash of thunder. He found it odd that there was no rain. But, even more so, he was bewildered by an unusual purple glow radiating from the sky. He saw this through the open door, and then he stepped outside. "What's going on?" he asked Lucifer, vigilantly, and then he noticed something astonishing that took place above his front yard – it was a whirlpool in the sky.

Lucifer trailed Drodz, and then observed the sky for himself. "This is not my doing." Although, the Devil was honest, he was also not daunted by the atmospheric disturbance. He was actually quite attuned with it.

Together, they witnessed the descent of the Angel of Death – a skeletal being in a black hooded cloak, best referred to as The Grim Reaper. When he reached the ground, the menacing figure stood approximately eight feet tall, with broad shoulders and armed with a dreadful scythe.

As Drodz gazed down from the fastening rift, he saw the Reaper eerily staring back at them from the foot of his yard.

Lucifer finally explained: "Apparently, the Grim Reaper does not tolerate unearthed corpses that wish to roam the land of the living."

"What?" Drodz shrieked, as he suddenly became devastatingly disappointed. He began to panic.

"Perhaps you should reconsider giving the dead

sovereignty."

The Reaper finally detached himself from his gaze, and then drifted away from the house.

"Where is he going?" Drodz worried.

"He's on his way to harvest your zombie, Viktor."

"No!"

Lucifer ran his fingernails across the wall and tore open a doorway for himself. But, before he returned to his world of darkness, Drodz cried, "Wait! If the Angel of Death manifests whenever I revitalize and free the deceased, then this jeopardizes my life's work!"

"Indeed. But, I would suggest that you re-evaluate your rationale before you decide to breach your contract. The penalty will be quite insufferable for you. I promise." Lucifer stepped into his dark province, and then the wall returned to its normal form.

CHAPTER 13:
THE HOMECOMING

Moments after his unsettling revelation, Ed found his way back to Warwick Road. But, he cringed to the sight of his own house; he knew that it was now cursed with malevolence. So, he stood still to prefigure the consequences of his return.

"Yo, Talbot!" shouted a familiar voice, and then Ed turned to see a few punks dressed as vampires. It was Owen who approached him, along with two of his thug-friends, armed with baseball bats.

Ed showed no fear. "What are you doing, Owen?"

"You're a dead man!" Owen threatened him.

"That's not funny."

As soon as Owen got close enough to Ed, he swung his bat and sent him to the ground. Ed played dead.

Owen and his thugs were surprised that they injured Ed so quickly and easily. They even became very concerned about his stillness.

"Hey, I don't think he's breathing, man," said one of the thugs.

"Of course he's breathing!" Owen told him, hesitantly.

The other thug kneeled down to find a pulse.

"I couldn't have killed him," Owen worried, and then his thug friend became paranoid.

"Holy shit!" his thug-friend shrieked, as he jumped to his feet.

"What?" Owen cried.

"You're gonna go to jail, man!"

Owen's so-called friends fled the scene and left him in the dust. But, when he turned back to Ed's body, he became terrified, and then decided to join his retreating friends.

* * *

Ed hid in his own garage and waited for the first ray of morning sunlight. At dawn, he spied through the windows and spotted his wife asleep in the master bedroom. Even as a dead man, he felt hatred. He was even sickened by the sight of Dr. Praetor asleep on *his* side of the bed.

He moved on to find Crystal, but her bedroom appeared to be vacant and untouched – he assumed that she could've spent the night with a friend. Ed would've been pleased to see his daughter again, but her absence encouraged his vindictive intentions.

Ed patiently waited for Lena and Praetor to wake up from the 7:00AM alarm. He set his enraged eyes on Lena as she reached over Praetor to turn off the alarm clock. She then kissed her rugged companion with unexpected bliss. As expected, she lured Praetor from his slumber and he quickly reciprocated. It was a lustful lovemaking, which only fueled Ed's resentment further.

When they eventually finished, Lena jumped in the shower, while Praetor got dressed and migrated to the living room. Ed stayed on him like a crazed predator. He watched him put on his overcoat and walk out the front door. He waited for Praetor to get inside his brand-new sports car and drive away, before he finally snuck inside his house.

By the time Lena stepped out of the shower and threw on a silk robe, Ed reached the master bedroom. He stood silently at the doorway and glared at her, as she attempted to deal with her hair at the vanity. It took a moment before she noticed her dead husband reflected in the mirror. She came to a petrified standstill and eventually screamed, "OH-MY-GOD! You're—! You're—!"

"Dead."

Lena launched off her seat and pressed up against the wall, as she gazed at Ed in disbelief. "You died! We're burying you!"

"Not anymore."

"When they brought you to the hospital you were dead-on-arrival. You cannot be alive!"

"I should be deceased, Lena. I know. But, I'm not. Usually, when blood ceases to pump through your body, you're a goner, right? But, not me – I'm a walking-talking corpse with only *one thing* on my mind, babe. Can you guess what that is?"

"Please," Lena wept, "don't kill me!" Then, she cried out for Praetor.

"Praetor left, sweetheart. And, I'm afraid that was his last house call."

Lena began to bawl in fear, as she slid down the wall.

As Ed began to approach her, he noticed the wind intensifying outside. And, when the house mysteriously began to flood with darkness, *he froze still.*

Without warning, the window suddenly exploded, along with some of the wall, and Lena was catapulted across the room. She fell face first at her dead husband's feet, and then Ed watched the Grim Reaper charge into the room.

"HOLY SHIT!" Ed shouted, in awe.

The Grim Reaper swung his scythe into Lena's back, and then hauled her up off the floor. Her final words were unintelligible screams, in reaction to the

Reaper, and then she was split in two!

In the midst of the blood shower, Ed saw the Reaper beckon him with his long, bony index finger. He knew that he was next, and then quickly escaped to the living room. But, as he hurried down the hall, the Reaper combusted into a blaze of sapphire flames, which quickly spread through the entire house. It trailed Ed to the front door, and then set the house off into an incredible inferno. The might of the explosion jolted Ed across the street. He landed on his neighbor's front lawn, and then watched his house burn to the ground.

Fortunately, his two-door garage was still intact. He swiftly evaded the bonfire to repossess one of his bikes, and then rode off before the fire department arrived. If he had an active heart, it would've been pounding out of his chest by now.

As he left Warwick Road once and for all, he was pleased to see that all of his probing neighbors were too fascinated with the firestorm than the sight of a dead man riding a motorcycle in the sunlight.

Even Drodz didn't notice him flee the scene, as he pulled up in his sedan to observe the catastrophe. He knew that the Grim Reaper was accountable, but he also believed that Ed could've survived. He continued his search.

CHAPTER 14:
DIA DE LOS MUERTOS

Ironically, it was the Day of the Dead in Mexico and, up in New York, Ed found himself attending his own funeral. He parked his bike and kept a considerable distance from his burial ceremony. He hid behind a mausoleum and eventually spotted his melancholy daughter in the midst of the crowd; and he saw that her girlfriend, Mandy, comforted her.

Ed also made an effort to find Gary, who stood beside his eye-candy assistant, Amy. But, when Gary excused himself to answer an incoming call on his vibrating cell, Ed moved in closer to eavesdrop. From what he could hear, he knew that Gary had received word of the unfathomable destruction of his home.

"Oh my God," Gary said into his cell. "Was Lena inside?" he asked, in shock, and then he listened to the caller's unheard response. "No, the daughter is here at the cemetery; she never went home. What caused it? Do you know?" He waited for a reply, and then said, "Okay, thanks, Lee. Well, let me know if you hear anything else. I'll be at my office for the rest of the day. I'll talk to you later." He pocketed his cell and returned to the conclusion of the burial.

After the Priest recited the final passage, each attendee – beginning with Crystal – was given a single rose to be placed on the coffin. "Goodbye, Daddy," Crystal wept, as she set her rose down. When she left the casket, she inadvertently walked in Gary's direction.

From Ed's position, he knew that Gary delivered the latest news to his daughter. Her unsettled reaction confirmed it, and then he watched her leave the cemetery, fed up.

When everyone paid their final valedictions with the roses, Ed returned to his motorcycle and eventually followed Gary back to the office.

* * *

Ed deliberately gave Gary enough time to get inside the office and settle in before he pursued him. When he did, he attempted to take the elevator up to the appropriate floor. But, it wasn't long before the elevator became unexpectedly jammed. It was an inconvenient twist of fate – or, perhaps, a premeditated action provoked by a mystical entity. At that point, Ed knew that anything could have been possible.

Nevertheless, he wasn't going to let a stalled elevator and a periodic light flicker get in his way. He hauled his ass through the overhead escape hatch. But, when he reached the top of the elevator, he sensed that something was amiss. He heard the sound of spectral wind flow throughout the elevator shaft. It was the same exact sound that he heard moments before the horrifying raid on his house.

In a panic, he physically ascended to the next level and lucratively forced the doors open to climb onto the desired floor. He then desperately attempted to locate Gary but, when he finally arrived at his friend's office, Gary was already resting in a pool of his own blood.

Ed cautiously drew near his slain colleague, with remorse. But, he knew that it was unwise to stand idle for too long. Therefore, he confiscated Gary's cell phone, and said farewell. "Forgive me, Gary."

As he stepped out of the blood-soaked office, he was struck in the face by a blast of tainted air. His eyes darted around, as he sensed the paranormal presence again. He cautiously walked down the hall and descended a stairwell. But, on his way down, he caught a glimpse of a dark, familiar figure climbing up from the first floor. He froze in a panic, and then spun around to return upstairs.

As Ed ran from the stairwell, the Grim Reaper appeared and sprinted after him. Ed found his way back to the inoperative elevator shaft and climbed down, carefully and hastily. He eventually noticed the Reaper peering down at him and was startled. Ed lost his grip, tumbled onto the stalled elevator, and then instantaneously dived back inside it.

The Reaper leaped onto the top, just as Ed closed the hatch, and then began to hack away with his scythe. The protruding blade nearly decapitated Ed, and then the elevator suddenly began to freefall. It crashed onto the first floor, and then Ed forced the doors open to escape.

As Ed ran out of the building, the Reaper successfully ripped his way into the decimated elevator, and then cleared his way into the reception area. But, by that time, Ed had already dashed out of the building and headed for his motorcycle.

Ed instantly started her up, and then sped away, as he saw Death storm out of the building.

He took the isolated industrial path toward the nearest outlet, but the Reaper gained on him and attempted to disable the bike with his scythe. Fortunately, Ed was able to outrun his dark pursuer by less than a foot. He abruptly hit the brakes and spun the bike 180-degrees, causing the Reaper to fly ahead of himself.

Ed quickly completed the u-turn and raced back the way he came. He noticed the Reaper standing still in the side-view mirror, and then watched the mystical creature transform into sapphire smog, which then seeped into the earth. "That can't be good," he said to himself, and then he saw the Angel of Death resurface from the ground ahead of him. He took a swing, but Ed successfully managed to dodge the scythe. However, his defensive maneuver caused him to lose control of the bike and he flung off.

Ed picked himself up and reunited with his bike, before the Reaper could reach him. He headed for another outlet and left the Reaper in his trail of dust. And, by the time Ed arrived to Main Street, the Reaper was no longer in pursuit.

CHAPTER 15:
FUGITIVE OF DEATH

Crystal wound up at the far end of Main Street, sulking at the quaint park that overlooked the Long Island Sound. She was on a bench, crying on Mandy's shoulder, and felt useless and miserable.

"There's nothing you could've done," Mandy consoled her.

"It's just too overwhelming, Mandy. First: my father, and now my mother."

"You don't know that; you're mother could've gotten out of the house in time – if she was even there."

Crystal sobbed in silence for a moment, and then hugged her friend. "Thank you for helping me through this. You and your family have been really great."

"It's my pleasure. My parents said that you could stay with us for as long as you have to."

After a while, Crystal regained some composure. "You should get to work before the new manager has a shit-fit."

"I know, but I'd hate to leave you like this."

"I'll be alright."

"I don't believe you."

"Believe me, I'll be right here when you finish your shift."

"Promise?"

"Cross my heart."

"Alright, but don't make me regret it."

"You won't," Crystal laughed, and then Mandy went to the coffeehouse on foot. But, on the way, she bumped into Owen, who had just stepped out of the deli. They exchanged a look of disgust, and then he turned to notice Crystal at the park.

The last thing Crystal needed was to be harassed by her ex-boyfriend.

"I thought you fell off the face of the earth," he told her, as he sat on the bench next to her. He offered her half of an Italian sub, but she ignored him.

"Leave me alone, please," she said, with an attitude. "Please! Thank you!"

But, Owen was relentless. "Look: I just wanted to say I'm sorry, okay!"

"Apology *denied*! Now, go away!"

"I'm sorry *for your loss*, Crystal. I heard about your father." He struck a nerve in Crystal, and then continued: "Did they find out who did it?"

"It was a hit and run! No, they don't know who the driver was."

Owen was confused. Apparently, he was still under the impression that *he* killed her father the night before. "Driver?" he asked. "He wasn't... beaten to death?"

She became emotionally disturbed. "Owen, I really just need to be alone right now. I *literally* just came back from the funeral!"

"Funeral?" he asked, confused. "Already?"

"Yes," she said, annoyed. "He died on Thursday! The wake was *last night* and *the funeral* was *this morning!*"

Owen began to freak out. "He died on... Thursday?"

Before Crystal could reply, an enraged Ed showed up by surprise and took Owen away. He dragged the punk by the hair and then threw him down a wooded hill. Owen fractured his collarbone as he tumbled downhill, near the water.

Crystal's jaw dropped, as she observed her living dead father chase after Owen. Ed dragged him into the shallow water, and then held his head beneath the surface until he finally stopped breathing.

As he rectified his vengeance, he turned to his petrified daughter who had let out an earsplitting scream. But, she was eventually silenced by the unexpected arrival of Drodz – he snuck up from behind to cover her mouth. "It's okay, darling," Drodz told her, softly. "It's okay."

"Get your fucking hands off her," Ed commanded, as he climbed up the hill.

"As you wish," Drodz said, and then Crystal collapsed, unconsciously. "I think it would be wise for us to converse some more, Edward."

"I think you're right," Ed told him; as he kneeled down to examine his daughter. He attempted to feel for her breath – or her heart rate – but no luck. "I can't feel shit!" he yelled, and then Drodz examined her for him.

"She's in shock," Drodz told him. "It's not every day someone gets to see their deceased parent return from the grave."

The wind mysteriously began to intensify, and then Ed became anxious. "I have to get away from here. There's a –"

"Yes, I know what hunts you. I'm afraid you're in great danger. Come; help me bring your daughter into my car. I'll explain everything."

Ed lifted Crystal from the ground, and then gently rested her in the backseat of Drodz's vehicle. Ed took the passenger seat, and then they drove off Main Street.

"Okay, Professor," Ed began, "*talk!*"

"From our initiation, I grasped that you knew a great deal about me – including my accord with Lucifer.

Yes?"

"Yes, but get to the point: what the hell does the Grim Reaper want with me? I mean: I'm already dead, right? So, what the fuck?"

In the midst of their conversation, Crystal silently awoke, but purposely remained hushed to listen to the outrageous dialogue in the front seat.

"A quarter of a century ago," Drodz began, "when Lucifer deceived me as some kind of wealthy chemist named 'Lewis,' he offered me a formula that endorsed perpetual life."

"And, you believed him?"

"Certainly not right away; but you must understand, it was a very desperate and traumatic time for me. I told him that I would do anything to have his remedy. The price, of course, was for me to deliver him the protracted souls that inhabit my victims. He took my wife's essence as an initial consignment, and then I tested my prize. I began with dead animals, and the results were exhilarating. So exhilarating that I became obsessed. I attempted to use the formula to save my brother from a fatal illness... and now you, from your unfortunate demise."

"So, what you're basically telling me is that... the Devil has my soul."

"Basically. Yes."

"That's wonderful," he said, sarcastically. "And, the Reaper is after me because...?"

"Because, you are a violation to the natural

world and it is forbidden for you to inhabit it. You're an escaped prisoner; a fugitive of death."

"Where am I supposed to go?"

"Six feet below, I'm afraid. You're an abomination, Edward. I've failed and now I am obligated to serve the Devil forever."

Ed stared at Drodz in an angry silence, and then he opened his mouth: "I don't know why, but I'd love to snap your neck right now. Why am I feeling these hostile tendencies all of a sudden? I actually murdered my daughter's asshole ex-boyfriend like it was nothing!"

"Perhaps a side-effect from the fluid that I implanted you with. It is not of this world."

"So, I'm hopped up on *Devil Juice*."

"In a manner of speaking, yes."

They were suddenly interrupted by Gary's ringing cell phone. Ed was pleased to see Lee's name displayed on the caller I.D. "Just the man I need to speak to," he said, and then answered the call: "I was just thinking about you... No, Gary *left town*... I'm an old friend. Listen: I really need to speak to you, Lee – *in person*. Where are you? ... Well, are you sitting down? ... This is Ed Talbot..." He began to speak louder: "Do you hear me now? This is ED TALBOT! I've got your mad scientist. Now, where the hell are ya?"

CHAPTER 16:
DISCLOSURE

Lee's headquarters was a garage-converted apartment obscured with an array of complex equipment: monitors, computers, radar, infrared – the works. His walls were plastered with strange notes and photographed ghost sightings. His work was undoubtedly an obsession.

As he anxiously awaited company, he readied his digital video camera, which he had setup in a corner for a candid recording. Then, when his guests appeared on his security monitor, he opened the door and greeted them with a flash from an SLR camera. The light bothered Drodz and Crystal, but Ed just stared back. "Do you mind? We're not here for an interview."

"Come on down." He led his company into his abode, and then discretely activated his hidden camcorder by remote. "So, can I get any of you something to eat or drink? I have a frozen dinner in the microwave; you're all welcome to it."

"Just some answers for now," Ed insisted.

"Sure, bro. Shoot."

"Well, for one: your abrupt tolerance to all of this is freaking me out a bit. Why?"

"You mean: why aren't I shocked? Well, because, Eddy, I inadvertently knew all about this. Especially when I saw Drodz at your wake, poking at your body. I tried to tell Gary, but he was too preoccupied to notice. By the way, where did you say Gary is? He left town?"

"Figuratively speaking," Ed said, mournfully. But, Lee was still confused.

"So, you're a ghost-seeker," Drodz presumed, after admiring Lee's dwelling.

"All my life," Lee said, proudly.

Drodz eventually spotted his wife's diary resting on a desk. "And, *a thief*! Explain yourself!"

"No problem, Professor. But, from the sound of it, I think your *science project* has some questions for me first."

"Look," Ed interjected toward Lee, "I am thrilled that you're stomaching my altered existence, but we really don't have time to chew the fat right now. I am in desperate need for your expertise."

"Talk to me, brother," Lee said.

"It's a long story, but I'm just gonna get to the point. There is a bad-ass phantom out there that wants to take me away."

"The personification of death," Drodz added.

"And," Ed continued, "I would need you to tell me how I can repel him. *Indefinitely*. I haven't had time to think straight yet and the son-of-a-bitch is like a teen-age horn dog on prom night."

Lee laughed, and then took a seat on one of his desk chairs. "Let me get this straight: *you die*, this dude *resurrects you* and now you want me to be your body-guard?"

"That's not exactly what I had in mind," Ed told him. "I need to fend off the Grim Reaper."

"And, deter the Devil," Drodz added.

"And, get my soul back from him," Ed added.

"Hey," Lee began, "don't get me wrong, I really appreciate what I'm hearing – *and seeing* – right now. Believe me. But, I'm not a security guard, fellas. I'm a paranormal investigator. I can locate specters for you, but not repel and deter them. I'm not an exterminator; I'm a writer and listener."

Drodz furrowed his brow. "How exactly are you compensated for this line of work?"

"Government grants," Lee grinned, as he began to snack on a bag of corn chips. He offered some to Drodz and Crystal, but they refused. "My website also has a decent fan base."

Ed recognized a strange list of names posted on the wall behind Lee and became interested.

Lee glanced back at the list. "Oh. That's just my *Witch List*."

"You mean...?" Ed began to ask.

"Yes, the *Hocus Pocus* witches – not a list of cruel women who refused to sleep with me," he told Ed, and then he remembered: "Well, that is actually how the list got started; I won't lie to you."

Ed noticed the name "Jade Barker" and then turned to see a candid photograph of her. "*This woman is a witch?*" he asked, in surprise.

"She wouldn't be there if she wasn't, man."

Drodz became very interested in the photograph, as well. "You know this woman?" he asked Ed.

"She was a client of mine. She tried to pull off a suicide scam with a life insurance policy. I thought she was a ditz, but she obviously knew what she was doing. Why, do you know her?"

He nodded before the words could escape his mouth. "She is my daughter," he confessed, warily.

Lee dropped his chips and quickly jotted the updated information in his memo book. "That actually makes sense!"

"In what way, Lee?" Ed inquired.

"It's all in Keira Drodz's diary!"

"My wife's book," Drodz enlightened. "Which your friend didn't seem to have any problem lifting from my home."

"Sorry, doc," Lee told him, "but, it's my job to uncover the unknown."

"It still does not give you the right to infringe my privacy!"

"What about the book?" Ed asked them, as he tried to remain focused.

"It was just a memoir," Drodz sighed.

"To say the least," Lee interposed, and then elaborated for Ed: "It's twenty-five percent diary, seventy-five percent handbook. There are more spells in there than in any other witch-book I've ever encountered. And, I've got news for you, professor, she unleashed all of your dark secrets."

"I suppose they're hardly secrets anymore," Drodz assumed.

"Maybe not to the people in this room, but – pardon the bluntness – that night you hacked your wife into pieces had a pretty interesting prelude. How you locked up your daughter in the attic, so you could kick the shit out of your wife until she was helplessly weak."

"Why must you continue to provoke me?" Drodz asked, angrily.

"There are blood stains on the damn entry! You signed a treaty with the Devil and sacrificed your wife for an immoral purpose. How do you live with yourself?"

"That's enough!" Drodz barked, and then he stormed toward the exit, irately. "I am not here to have my past put on trial. Edward seems to believe that you would be able to support him. But, clearly, you are nothing but a worthless, thieving human being!"

"Easy, doc. You're misinterpreting me here. I'm not a confrontational guy, but I think I could actually be of service."

"Please, Lee," Ed implored. "Anything."

Lee grabbed the diary and flipped through the pages. "This is a book of charms, curses and hexes. I'm sure we could find something in here that could form – I don't know – some kind of *mystical blockade* or some shit."

"Neither of you were appointed to channel any of that material," Drodz said.

"Were you?" Ed asked.

"I am only capable of achieving hypnotic spells. Anything that deals with materialization is beyond my ability."

"Keira Drodz was a witch, Eddy," Lee said, "and, Jade Barker is the fruit of her womb. She could get the job done for ya."

Before Ed could answer, he became distracted by an unusual pulsing sound intensifying from the radar system. A large mass appeared to be drawing near the center of the electronic display.

Lee became obsessed with it, and then checked his other monitoring systems, which all revealed similar results. Something unnatural was out there. It wasn't too far, and it moved rapidly. "What did you say was after you, Eddy?"

"Death."

"I think we're in deep shit."

"Why? What is it?"

"This *thing* appeared on my radar screen the night of your wake. It's been on and off ever since. And, now, the fucking thing is headed right for my apartment. I can't imagine what else it could possibly be."

"Then," Ed began, sternly, "I recommend we go find Jade before your headquarters gets obliterated. I know where she lives."

"That's good to know, but she wouldn't be home tonight. Not at this hour."

"Okay, genius, then where the hell would she be?"

"It's Saturday night on Halloween weekend. She's where all of the local Witch and Goth types go. Valeria's Cauldron."

CHAPTER 17:
THE ALLIANCE

Valeria's Cauldron was a nightclub hidden in the industrial park, not far from where Ed once worked. It catered exclusively to the Goth crowd, so Lee made sure that he and his party were dressed appropriately. Ed and Drodz wore black overcoats; and Crystal, although temporarily mute, played along and went heavy with her eye shadow – Lee also supplied her with a fake I.D. card. And, Lee himself had dressed up in a jet-black suit. They were a band of oddities and blended in nicely.

Goth clubbers from all over the tri-state area were present that evening and the dance floor hopped to the ominous techno-beats governed by the creepy Disc Jockey. It was quite an experience for all of them – except for Lee, who had a tendency to drop in on occasion.

"How do you expect to find Jade in this?" Ed shouted to Lee, over the loud music.

Lee checked his watch, and then confidently told Ed, "Two minutes." Of course, Ed and Drodz were confused by his answer.

But, after two minutes had passed, the creepy D.J. made an enthusiastic announcement: "Ladies and gentlemen! Boils and ghouls! Throw your eyes on the stage and put your hands together for *RAVEN!*"

The crowd exploded with cheer and applause, as they all faced the stage to gawk at an exotic dark haired beauty. It was Jade, scarcely clad and performing an erotic dance to an intoxicating beat. The audience went wild over her.

"She's an exotic dancer too?" Ed asked.

"You'll see," Lee smiled.

Behold, a microphone stand ascended from the floor, as the stage began to flood with artificial smoke. As Jade approached the microphone, a live band appeared behind her – a drummer, guitarist, bass player and keyboard artist. As the music took a spin into a steady, dark rhythm, Jade began to sing:

In the realm of darkness came a shattered light. It came from the land of day and night.

It soared through clouds and conquered the mountains. It dove into hell and drank blood from the fountains.

*In the realm of darkness the light found her and said,
Please show me mercy for I am not dead.*

*The light took her hand and glided away. Adrift in
the tunnels to lie and sway.*

In the realm of darkness the light feared and cried.

In the realm of darkness the light faded and died.

Jade stepped backward, away from the micro-phone, as the band concluded their song, "In the Realm of Darkness," with an incredible jam session. The spot-lights blacked out and the crowd roared and cheered.

Lee quickly led the gang backstage, where they found Jade in a corridor. She was perspiring and inat-tentive, and wanted nothing more than her cold bottle of water. But, when Lee approached her, with all smiles, she gave him a loathsome look.

"That was amazing!" Lee complimented her.

Without speaking a word, Jade forcefully grabbed Lee by the lapels and pressed a long, lustful kiss against his lips. Ed compulsively covered his daughter's eyes until they were finished and, when they were, Jade punched Lee's dazed face with a solid right.

"Aw, shit!" Lee cried.

"I take it you two actually know each other," Drodz assumed.

"We used to date," Lee told him.

For the first time in her adulthood, Jade recog-nized her father and, with abrupt fury, she threw her water bottle at him. "You son-of-a-bitch!" she screamed, and then attempted to physically attack and murder Drodz with her bare hands. But, Lee quickly recovered from the sucker punch and restrained her from behind. "Get your fucking hands off of me! I can't believe you brought him here, you asshole!!!" She went hysterical over Drodz. "Die! Die! Die!" She balled in Lee's arms.

"Jade, relax!" Lee said. "It's alright." He hugged her, "It's alright, Jade. Shhh."

Jade regained her composure, and then spit in Lee's face. He let her lose, allowing her to storm into her dressing room.

"I guess you should've waited outside," Ed thought, to Drodz.

"Hindsight's twenty-twenty," Lee interjected, and then he guided Ed to Jade's dressing room, where she changed into something *warmer.*

"You're unbelievable, Lee," she said, disdainfully.

"Thank you," he smiled, sarcastically.

"You seduce me a few times, and then cheat on me with your ridiculous job; and now, you return to my life with the man who ruined it. I curse the air you breathe."

"Once again," Lee whispered to Ed, "another person who misinterprets me."

"What's *he* doing here?" Jade asked, referring to Ed.

"Actually, Jade," Lee began, "Ed is the reason why I'm here – it has nothing to do with your father. Well, in a way, it kinda does. But, not really."

Jade approached Ed, as if she were suddenly attracted to him. "You look different."

"I changed my lifestyle," Ed said, wryly.

"I would've never predicted to see you again – and, at the Cauldron, of all places."

"I was just dying to see you."

Lee couldn't resist interrupting them with a sarcastic remark: "Were you this funny before you died?"

"Died?" Jade asked, as she took a cautious step back. "What do you mean?"

"Jade," Lee began to ask. "How much would you say you *really* know about your father?"

"He had something to do with the death of my mother and he abandoned me. I grew up with deceitful, abusive guardians and that's why I hate him so much. No offense, Lee, but I didn't bother to read much into your articles on the subject."

"Well, then you should probably read this," he replied, as he handed Jade her mother's diary.

Jade opened it and right away knew what it was. It was an overwhelming moment that slowly began to answer her life's mystery.

Lee continued to explain, as she explored her mother's book. "You see: all of that hearsay about your father's plan to cure death was actually true. Ed here is *living proof* – well, sort of. He died the day before Halloween, but your father kept him out of the grave."

She heard Lee's words, but the diary dominated her attention. It revealed the romantic past between her parents, which eventually leaped into an era of wicked-ness. It spoke of the chemist named Lewis Sypher – the man who made a deal with her father, but also deceit-fully seduced her mother. Jade learned how Lucifer turned her parents against each other and how, under possession, Drodz committed the unspeakable acts that he's been paying for. The revelation forced tears from Jade's eyes, as she experienced genuine sympathy for the first time. She collapsed on a chair, and then saw her father at the threshold of her dressing room.

"Not a day has passed by without me thinking of you," Drodz told her, sincerely.

Jade jumped into her father's overdue embrace and wept with joy. "I am so sorry!" she sobbed. "Please forgive me! Please…"

"It's alright, child. We will soon find a way to heal the past."

During their sentimental moment, Lee checked his pulsating tracking device and saw trouble. "Shit! We have to get out of here right now!"

"What's going on?" Jade asked, confused. But, before anyone could answer, the building began to tremble and screams of agony were heard from the dance floor.

Crystal ran in, even more petrified than before, but she spoke: "There's something here!" she warned.

Ed and Lee quickly ran down the corridor to have a look at the dance floor. The others followed and they witnessed a gruesome massacre! The Grim Reaper slashed through the crowd with his scythe; blood and guts splattered everywhere. It was heretical. The Angel of Death was persistent and wrathful. Nobody made it out of the club in one piece – and, those who did bled to death before reaching their cars.

This was a first for Jade, Crystal and Lee. The women were stunned, but Lee had the audacity to use his camera phone to take a photo. Unfortunately, the flash drew attention and the Reaper stared them down. It pointed Ed out, as it did once before, and then began to charge after them.

"You fucking idiot!" Ed yelled at Lee, as they all began to run down the corridor in a panic.

"I didn't realize I had the flash on!" Lee yelled, defensively. "I didn't even know these things *had* flashes!"

"Is there a back way out of here?" Drodz asked his daughter.

"Yes! Just follow me!" she cried.

"Drodz," Ed began, "whatever happens, don't let that thing finish me until my soul is out of the Devil's hands!"

Behind them, the Reaper plowed through the wall and then continued to pursue the ill-fated team. But, as they finally reached the back exit, the Reaper drew closer and irrevocably captured Ed.

"No!" Drodz shouted.

But, Ed didn't give in. He struggled with the Reaper, as it carried him through the roof and into the night sky. "DON'T LET HIM FINISH ME!" he shouted, as his voice faded away.

"Daddy!" Crystal screamed at the top of her lungs.

"The cemetery!" Drodz cried. "We have to get to the cemetery! The Reaper is going to return him to his grave!"

With that said, the remaining group hurried outside and piled into Lee's car. They instantly headed for Matheson Cemetery.

"It has never been attempted before," Drodz began, to Jade, "but your mother had a spell in that book that could generate a rift in time and space. If you have the power to summon it, we just might be able to purge the Reaper from this world."

"It sounds like a great plan, doc," Lee said. "But, what if it fails?"

"Then, we lose Edward Talbot permanently and spend the rest of our short lives evading the Reaper's rampage."

"So, in other words: we have no choice," Lee realized.

"Correct."

Jade quickly found the spell in her mother's diary and book-marked it. "I've never summoned anything before," she confessed to her father.

"I believe in you, sweetheart."

CHAPTER 18:
FEARING THE REAPER

Lee pulled up to the cemetery gates, and the gang quickly climbed out of his car. The Iron Gate was locked, so they followed Drodz's lead and climbed over it. "Child," he began to ask Crystal, "Do you know where they buried your father?"

"Yes," she answered, and then led them all to it.

But, when they eventually had the tombstone in sight, they halted in a panic. They were too late. The Grim Reaper had just finished planting Ed's corpse and Drodz was actually surprised to see that Ed's grave was near his wife's. But, he was more concerned about the Reaper sensing their unwelcome presence. "Sweetheart," he began to tell his daughter, "I need you to get to that cathedral and recite that incantation. You two go with her."

"What are *you* gonna do?" Lee asked.

"I'm going to get Ed, and then we're going to lead the Reaper into the cathedral and ram that bastard into oblivion. Now, go!"

Jade, Lee and Crystal ran toward the cathedral. The Reaper noticed, and then began to soar after them. Drodz took advantage of the Reaper's distraction and ran up to rescue Ed from his grave.

As soon as Jade, Lee and Crystal reached the cathedral doors, the Reaper landed in the midst of a nearby cluster of graves.

"It's locked!" Lee shouted, referring to the doors.

"Well, just try to open it!" Jade replied, and they all began to pound on the door.

"What's he doing?" Crystal whimpered, as she noticed the Reaper's strange behavior.

"I don't know!" Lee shouted. "Just help me open the doors!"

The Reaper eventually slammed his staff into the ground, creating an enormous tremor. The shockwave actually helped them open the cathedral, and they quickly ran inside and closed the doors behind them. Jade immediately ran up to the altar to commence the séance, and Crystal peered out the window, while Lee began to barricade the doors with pews.

Crystal witnessed the power of the Grim Reaper,

as all of the surrounding graves unleashed their de-composed bearers. The dead awoke. Crystal screamed at the top of her lungs, rousing Lee and Jade to have a look themselves.

"I've got a bad feeling about this!" Lee shouted, and then Jade quickly returned to the altar, in a panic.

Zombies began to march up to the abandoned structure, as the Reaper gazed in satisfaction.

* * *

When Drodz arrived to Ed's resting place, he found himself staring at his wife's nearby tombstone for a moment. He sighed, and then, without further ado, he dug Ed out. It wasn't long before he found his lifeless, jittery hands. He grasped them and pulled with all his might.

Ed's head eventually resurfaced, and then he spewed a glob of dirt. "What took you so long?" Ed joked, and then attempted to help himself out.

As Drodz stepped back, Keira's corpse tore out of the earth and began to drag her husband into the grave with her! He shrieked in terror, and then reached out for Ed's help. But, Ed wasn't completely out of the ground yet, and therefore was of no use.

Drodz struggled and squirmed, as Keira pulled him into her grave. He relentlessly cried for help, until the ground eventually claimed his life.

By the time Ed was able to resurface entirely, he was too late. He lost his friend. "No!" he gasped, and then he was suddenly taken by surprise when the Reaper attacked him. Death swung his scythe and managed to lop off Ed's left-hand, which then rolled downhill.

In a panic, Ed quickly dodged the Reaper and scurried after his tumbling hand. He swiped it up and placed it in his pocket. Then, he managed to hide behind several mausoleums. But, he knew that wherever he hid had to be temporary. He also knew that his dark hunter walked the path beyond the burial chambers; he sensed his mystical energy. "Look," Ed began to communicate with the Reaper, "I don't understand why you're so obsessed with the rules of paranormal society, but these are different times, Grim. If a dead man wants to take a walk, let him take a walk!"

Ed suddenly became distracted when he heard his daughter cry for help. He soon realized that she was trapped in that cathedral, surrounded by flesh eating zombies. "Holy shit," he said, under his breath, and then the Reaper leaped over the nearest mausoleum. Ed avoided the swinging scythe and ran toward the invaded cathedral.

The Reaper flew after him with immense fury.

* * *

The zombies were about to break through the gothic structure when Jade was on the brink of completing the spell. Lee and Crystal took whatever they could find – mostly large crosses and candle sticks – to fend off the intruding zombies.

"Daddy!" Crystal shrieked, as she noticed her father through the window, running from the Reaper.

"Hurry, Jade!" Lee shouted. "When they get to the cathedral, I'm gonna open these doors!"

A storm miraculously took shape outside, but wind began to circle the altar. Jade's eyes turned white. She completed the chant: "*Shalladok, Darios, Zandellar!*" And then the wind transformed into an enormous vortex. It was a horizontal cyclone that swallowed everything that wasn't secure. Jade quickly held onto an ivory table, while Crystal and Lee clasped the opening doors. Everything outside, beginning with the ferocious zombies, was sucked into the rift like loose particles into a vacuum.

Ed found himself lifted off the ground and was weightlessly carried into the cathedral. Crystal grabbed his only hand, as he passed the threshold and held onto him tightly.

The Reaper saw what he was up against, and attempted to use his might against the rift's pull. But, he was beaten. The vortex dragged him into the cathedral, but he latched his bony hands onto the frame of the entrance. He persisted to struggle with the gravitational flux.

"Shut it off!" Ed shouted. "Shut it off, before we all die!"

"It won't stop until Death passes through it!" Jade shouted, over the screaming cyclone.

It wasn't until a bolt of lightning struck an old tree just outside the cathedral, which detached from it's dying roots. It hurtled into the Reaper's back and forced him down the aisle. But, before he reached the swirling, opaque whirlpool, he managed to snatch Ed from Crystal's grasp.

"NOOOOO!" Crystal cried, as she watched her father rocket through the void with the Grim Reaper, until they were no longer visible. She lost her grip and drifted toward the dying rift, but as it finally evaporated she fell to the floor. The wind and the raging storm were over and done with. "Bring him back!" Crystal ordered Jade, as tears poured from her eyes. "Bring him back! Please, bring him back!"

Jade approached Crystal to comfort her. "We can't, sweetie… I'm sorry."

"No, no, no!" she continued to cry, and then hugged Jade tightly.

Lee stood by with regret and believed that they had actually failed. The Reaper may have been gone, but Ed wasn't meant to share his fate.

In the land of the living, the legend of Dead Ed Talbot had come to an end. But, on *the other side*, it merely just began.

CHAPTER 19:
THE DEVIL'S PLAYGROUND

Ed found himself resting on the sofa of his childhood home and everything was exactly the same as his reoccurring nightmare. His mother was preparing dinner in the kitchen, the old cartoons were on the television and the two deformed ghosts stood in the center of the hallway. The only difference was that Ed was his 43-year-old self and this experience was authentic.

"Come with us," said one of the phantoms, as it waved Edward over to them. But, instead of running away, Ed challenged his fear and entered the eerie hallway. He pierced through the apparitions, opened the closet door, and then beheld a staircase to darkness.

He confidently descended into the dark void, as the staircase spiraled down an infinite abyss. It took a while, but Ed eventually discovered the rock-strewn floor. He then wandered down a cavern tunnel and eventually arrived to an outdoor vile landscape. Strange electrical storms filled the blood red sky and strong gusts of wind swirled around him.

Ed decided to search the rocky badlands for answers. And, as he trekked across the harsh environment, he eventually came to a stop near a great round gap in the land. He peered into it and witnessed an outlandish spherical object ascend to the surface. When it drew near, Ed quickly took a step back, and then became aware of dozens of other pits – just like the one he found – in the surrounding area.

The ground began to tremble, as more colossal spheres emerged from the chasms, simultaneously. They encircled Ed; he didn't know what to think of it. He became frightened, yet he was brave enough to examine the sphere before him. In it, he saw – and heard – suffering, suspended souls. As he gazed intently, he eventually noticed Drodz's spirit, which then unexpectedly pressed up against the inner walls of the sphere.

"Drodz!" Ed gasped.

"Help me!" Drodz begged, and then he was heaved away by Keira's irritated soul.

This intensified Ed's fear and compelled him to run back to the cavern. But, he was lost and took off into the dark distance, unintentionally.

When he arrived to the frontier of a mysterious bleak forest, he decreased his running speed and began to walk the rest of the way. But, just before he entered the woodland, he suddenly heard loud, boorish laughter – and it wasn't human or friendly. He glanced over his shoulder to see a gang of small, wicked creatures – *demons* – dragging fresh souls toward the spheres.

Unfortunately, they were not oblivious to Ed's unwelcome presence. In fact, some of the demons decided to chase after him with burning limbs.

Ed panicked and continued to run, as the demons began to gain on him.

When he finally entered the forest, he found the bulkiest tree to hide behind. Curiously, the demons were reluctant to enter the forest. It was as if they feared it. So, they returned to their dealings in the outskirts.

Poor Ed didn't know what to do. He feared the mystifying forest, but he also feared everything outside of it. Although, after a brief moment of hesitation, Ed soon decided to stay put in the forest and move onward.

He cautiously hiked through the woods, but at one point managed to trip over a rock and took a tumble down a steep hill.

He landed in a vaporous bog! And, as soon as he struck the marshland, a pair of decomposed hands tore out of the mud and fastened Ed to the ground.

He frantically tried to remove the ruthless corpse

hands. As he struggled to break free, he noticed that the sludgy surface up ahead began to gush and simmer.

Suddenly, an enormous beast emerged from the bubbling muck and it stood nearly fifteen-feet tall!

Ed panicked, as he witnessed the behemoth let out a great, disturbing growl.

It immediately began to advance him, but Ed suddenly managed to break loose and scurry away, before the great beast was able to swipe him.

Ed ran as fast as he could, mindful of what was pursuing him, until he returned to the barren outskirts. He eventually came to a complete halt and found himself face-to-face with Drodz, in that sphere that inhabited him. Ed's toes barely touched the edge of the chasm beneath it.

Drodz's spirit saw the behemoth gallop from the forest behind Ed. Before it reached them, Drodz managed to pierce through the translucent skin of the sphere and grabbed Ed by his collars. "This is no place for you!" he warned, and then he attempted to pull Ed closer to the edge, but Ed resisted – Ed didn't trust anything in this netherworld anymore, not even his own friend's soul. However, the fearsome roar of the approaching beast startled Ed enough to lose his balance, which then allowed Drodz to pull him over the abyss. "Save your soul!" Drodz warned Ed.

"Where is it?"

"You must confront Lucifer! You mustn't allow him to include it in this dreadful entrapment!" Drodz cried, and then released his grip. "SAVE YOUR SOUL!" he yelled, as he watched Ed plummet into the pits of hell.

When Ed eventually struck the surface, he found himself in the heart of Lucifer's lair. He picked himself up and saw the lord of darkness staring back at him from his throne. "Lucifer, I presume."

"Edward Talbot," Lucifer grinned. "Welcome. I must commend you; no gatecrasher has ever survived the wasteland before."

"Well, one would have to be alive in order to survive, wouldn't you say?"

Lucifer was amused. "Even a zombie has an obligation to survive, Edward. And, I must say, I am impressed. Perhaps you could be of service to me after all."

"How about we skip the sweet talk and get right to the point? You have something that I want."

"What I have is no longer yours to reclaim."

"What you have was never anyone else's to give!"

Lucifer stood up and approached Ed. "Nevertheless, what's done is done and you are out of luck, my friend. Mother Nature will reject you in the land of the living; Heaven will deny you without a soul; and if you refuse my offer, you will certainly suffer down here. You have no value."

"So, in other words, you give me no choice."

"Oh, but there is a choice: *serve* or *suffer*. So,

what's it going to be?"

"If I serve you, what exactly will I gain in return?"

"Existence."

"I'm afraid that won't cut it."

"Oh?"

"You see: since I've died, I've hated what I've become. To be honest with you, I'd love to end it right now. But, I'm not gonna rest easy. Not until I know that my soul is in a better place."

"It is unwise of you to bargain with me, Edward."

"Yeah, well I don't really give a shit; I'm fucking dead!"

Lucifer considered it. "One hundred years."

"Of service?"

"Take Drodz's place as my *soul catcher* for one hundred years, and I will release your life-force."

"What, hand you thousands of souls for the sake of saving just one? I tell you what: I'll give you *one* soul in exchange for mine."

"One soul is not an option."

"Well, it's my final offer."

"You have a lot of nerve for a soulless piece of flesh!"

"I have nothing to lose."

Lucifer remained angrily silent, and then Ed stepped out of the lair and into another chamber. But, he had nowhere specific to go. Eventually, he managed to get himself cornered on the edge of a great cliff, which led to another chasm. Several of those ferocious little creatures from the outside had emerged from the shadows and moved toward him. They ultimately managed to drive him over the edge, and then Ed fell onto an ascending sphere. He held on tightly, as it lifted toward another canal.

Lucifer approached the boundary of the cliff to spot Ed escaping on one of his detention-orbs. They locked eyes, until Ed and the sphere disappeared into a higher level.

As Ed elevated toward the light above – which he knew led to the wasteland – he suddenly found himself face-to-face with *his own soul!* As fate would have it, it was suspended in the sphere that carried him and Ed frantically attempted to "save himself." But, the sphere was impossible to breach. Eventually, his soul caught on, and attempted to break through from the inside. There were no results and they both grew frustrated. Ed grunted and bellowed, as he punched, scratched and stomped on the exterior, but nothing worked. Eventually, the other trapped spirits noticed and assisted Ed's soul, in a desperate attempt to break free.

As they hovered outside, into the wasteland, Ed wailed at the top of his decaying lungs until the screaming souls were finally able to rupture the sphere. They launched into the unnatural sky, blaring in victory. It was a rewarding experience for Ed, as he watched the fortunate souls break out of Hell. He laughed loudly and cheered their triumphant escape.

At last, his soul was free. But, his zombie self was still a nomad stranded in Hell.

Suddenly, the Devil – in his winged, monstrous form – soared out of the chasm and captured Ed. He carried him toward a rocky region, and then slammed him into a gritty partition. Ed slid to the gravelly surface, and then began to throw rocks at the airborne Devil.

"Come on!" Ed dared. "You want a piece of me, come on!!!"

The Devil was furious. He dived in an attack position, but Ed ran off toward that dreaded dark forest before he could reach him.

He raced through the swampland, with the Devil in aerial pursuit, and then found that damn behemoth again. It roared in fury and then halted, as the Devil descended in his manlike form. Ed was surrounded.

"It's a shame I no longer have your soul. I would've taken great pleasure in shredding it apart."

"You've lost, Lucifer."

"Oh, no, Edward. Vengeance is a luxury that I never neglect. You may be lifeless, but I know what drives you. *Your daughter* will soon suffer the punishment that you deserve."

"NO!" Ed shouted, as he attempted to attack Lucifer. But, before he could reach him, he found himself lifted from the ground by his own soul. It carried him away from the Devil's land.

Lucifer became enraged, and then quickly trans-formed back into his winged form to fly after his adver-sary. But Ed and his soul prevailed, as they outran the Devil in the sky and penetrated the barrier of Hell. The Devil paused in midair and emitted an odious snarl.

CHAPTER 20:
VENGEANCE

Dr. Praetor became very depressed when he learned what had happened to the Talbot residence. Lena was presumed dead and the media was under the impression that it was suicide. But, Praetor knew that it wasn't true. If anything, the death of her husband made her happier than ever.

But, to deal with his depression, Praetor deliberately worked late hours at the Cromwell Psychiatric Center. He felt that his work would keep him occupied. But, midnight was his limit.

When he entered the vacant parking garage to locate his car, he heard someone call his name:

"Are you Dr. Praetor?" asked the voice.

Praetor turned and saw Lee, who stood coolly near a staircase. "Who wants to know?" Praetor asked.

"The name's Lee Cushing. My cousin Emma used to be your secretary – before she quit. *You know*: from your sexual harassment problem."

Praetor suddenly felt uncomfortable. "What can I do for you, Mr. Cushing?"

"Actually, it's what *I* can do for *you*."

"I don't understand."

"Of course you don't; I haven't explained it to you yet."

Praetor sighed in annoyance. "Sir, please, it's late. If you have something to tell me, spit it out so I can be on my way."

"It's about your old friend, Viktor Drodz. He passed away last night."

"I'm sorry to hear that."

"I understand he told you all about his *cure*, didn't he?"

"Ravings of a lunatic. Nothing more."

"Oh, but it's true, doctor. I've seen the results."

"The theory to reanimate the dead is absurd!"

"Would you like to see proof?"

"I don't have to. I know it's a sham."

"But, you're wrong."

Praetor hesitated, and then furrowed his brow. "Who are you again?"

Lee handed him a business card. "Lee Cushing –

paranormal investigator and freelance writer for the Arkanville Press. Drodz was a hobby of mine."

"I see. Okay, Mr. Cushing. How can you prove me wrong?"

"I can show you his laboratory."

"Okay," Praetor laughed. "Show me his laboratory."

* * *

Lee led Praetor to Drodz's residence, and then lured him into the subterranean lab.

"My god," Praetor gasped. "He was genuinely obsessed."

"*Passionate* was more like it," Lee suggested.

Praetor explored the lab, and then eventually came across Drodz's journal. He was amazed by the contents and illustrations. "Alright," he said. "So, he was obviously onto something here. But, what about the chemist who provided him with the missing elements?"

"You mean: *Lucifer*."

"Well, the man called himself Lewis Sypher. But, who was he really?"

"He was the embodiment of Satan," Ed said, as he stepped out of the shadows.

Praetor turned to stone. "It can't be," he gasped.

"Oh, it *be*," Ed said, as he approached Praetor, sinisterly. "You took my life away, Praetor. And then your former patient gave it back to me. Kinda uncanny, wouldn't ya say?"

"But, you died! We killed you!"

"And, I missed you at my funeral."

"This is impossible!"

"Well, if you believed Drodz, then you should know that it *is* possible."

"It can't be!" Praetor shrieked, and then turned to Lee. "You tricked me!"

"Yes and no," Lee told him. "You wanted the proof. *Ed* is the proof."

"Tell me, *Dr. Praetor*," Ed began to ask. "Do you believe in the death penalty?"

Praetor knew what Ed was implying. So, he punched Lee out of his way, and then escaped the laboratory.

Ed furiously pursued him out of the house.

As Praetor returned to his car, he immediately locked the windows and started her up. But, as he took off, Ed managed to jump on the back. He quickly climbed to the roof, and then leaned over the windshield to punch a hole through it. He grabbed Praetor by the neck, and then he slammed on the brakes to force Ed off the hood and onto the street.

Praetor slammed on the gas and ran him over at 50-miles per hour. He thought he had beaten him, but Ed had actually grabbed onto the bottom of the car. It wasn't easy with just one hand, but he managed to pull himself up alongside the passenger-door. When he reached the window, he busted through and attacked

Praetor!

The car spun out of control and into a ditch, but it finally stopped when it crashed into a tree. Praetor quickly escaped the wrecked vehicle, with his face drenched in his own blood. He attempted to climb out of the trench with a limp, and then Ed went after him.

"Please!" Praetor cried. "I'll give you anything! I'll give you money!"

"Now, what would a dead man like me need with money?"

"You don't have to do this!"

"You're right. But, *I want to.*"

The wind suddenly began to pick up and a vortex appeared in the sky, right above the ditch. It began to inhale everything – just as it did at the cemetery.

Praetor grabbed a tree branch, but then Ed seized him and broke his arm. Praetor screamed in agony as he lost his grip, and then the rift swallowed him and Ed.

"Say goodbye, bub!" Ed shouted, and then he laughed until they vanished with the vortex.

Jade appeared at the top of the ditch, as she closed her mother's diary. Lee eventually joined her and they gazed at the empty night sky.

"Do you think he'll come back?" Lee asked her.

"He did before, didn't he?"

* * *

Ed returned to Lucifer's lair and presented Praetor at

his throne.

"What's this?" Lucifer asked.

"Unlike you," Ed began, "I'm a man of my word. This is William Praetor – the man who stole my wife and murdered me for her. I'm sure you two will get along just fine."

Lucifer was impressed with Ed's veracity. He respectfully waited for him to leave, before he unleashed his hungry demons on Praetor. They tore him to shreds and devoured his innards.

EPILOGUE:
THE AFTERMATH

By the end of the month, Lee posted an editorial on his website titled "Restless In Peace," which was essentially Ed's story. It explained the entire calamity that police officials attempted to figure out on their own. But, of course, like any other stranger absent from the preceding supernatural events, they were skeptical of Lee's story. Although, till this day, police are still uncertain of the many unanswered questions:

Who demolished the Talbot house?

Where did the bodies of Lena Talbot and Dr. William Praetor go?

What happened to Viktor Drodz?

Who murdered Gary Walker?

What happened to all of the corpses at Matheson Cemetery?

The list went on and on, and nobody in their right mind accepted Lee's testimony.

And, Lee wasn't even looking for a profit. He just felt that the story had to be told – not only to prove his research, but to also commemorate his friend, Edward Talbot.

Crystal appreciated Lee's efforts, but swore herself to secrecy. She promised herself to never speak of the supernatural events to anyone for as long as she lives. Yet, she had befriended Jade, so she is bound to experience similar dealings at some other time.

Lee made it a point to check up on them from time to time. His views on witchcraft had finally become liberated, and he supported Crystal's interest in learning the art of necromancy – in hopes that she would one day communicate with her father. But, communicating with the dead was far simpler than Lee had thought.

After he reviewed his first batch of email responses to his latest article, he received a text-message on his cell phone from an unknown number. The message read: "THANKS, LEE" and he replied with: "WHO IS THIS?"

The response was surprisingly prompt: "YOU KNOW WHO THIS IS."

Lee smiled, and then almost laughed in surprise when he realized the possibility of Ed being on the other end. So, he wrote back: "ED? IS THAT YOU?"

"HOW'S MY DAUGHTER?" he replied.

"SHE'S SAFELY IN THE COMPANY OF WITCHES. LOL. WHERE ARE YOU?"

"TELL HER THAT I LOVE HER AND THAT I WILL ALWAYS BE WITH HER."

"I WILL. BUT, WHERE ARE YOU?"

"BE GOOD, LEE. SEE YOU IN 60-YEARS."

Lee chuckled, and then typed his final response: "SAVE ME A SEAT."

And then, Ed was gone.

Edward M. Talbot
1965-2008

AFTERWORD

This was the first of many tales to take place in the haunted village of Arkanville.

Lee Cushing, Jade Barker and Crystal Talbot will return.

M. P.

ACKNOWLEDGEMENTS

Special Thanks to My Family: *Mom, Dad, Ronnie, Debbie Joe, Jessica, Sadie, Jerry, Mike, Andy, Tommy, Carlene, Christine, James, Matt, Ross, Jean, Melanie, Ray, Lance, John, Audra E., Amanda, Brandon, Jordan, Danny, Devin, Emily, Leah, Kimberly, Danielle, Joy, Jason, Audra D., Logan, Laura, Tony, Dolores, Paul, Nicole, Joe T., Anita, the Tucciarone family, the DiMaggio family, the Bryant family, the Pita family, the Badami family.*

My Friends: *Jason, Maureen, Harry, Scotty, Randy, Ray, Christine, Mike, Randal, Carol, Steve, David, Lindella, "Mama" Lindella, Joshua, Chloe, the Perry Family, the Napolitano family, the Nowak family, the Waldorf Family & the Waldorf Staff.*

ABOUT THE AUTHOR

Mike Polizzi is an aspiring screenwriter turned novelist. Born in 1977, Mike was raised, and continues to reside, in Suffolk County, Long Island. He has contributed his talents in both independent films and the corporate world.